ADAM'S CANE

Jon Ferguson

You say you want truth.
What you want is your truth.

Huge Jam Publishing, 2022
www.hugejam.com

ISBN: 978-1-911249-95-5

To Raymond Pittet

who hired me for my first writing job

at "Le Matin" forty-two years ago.

PART I

I wake up every morning between four and four-thirty with a stiffy. Usually it is four-twenty, but sometimes it's a bit earlier or later. It takes ten or fifteen minutes for the log to melt, then another half hour to get back to sleep. Sometimes I read, sometimes I lie in the dark next to my softly purring girlfriend. She isn't the type I can wake up with a few fingers between the thighs. Not anymore, anyway. She has to get up at six for work and relieving my aching joint at such hours isn't part of her weekly – or yearly – agenda. Even this morning it happened and my father's funeral is this afternoon. He died four days ago when his lungs stopped working. I wasn't there, but that's what the nurse said. "He went ('il s'en est allé')," she said, "between four and five." Just when I was being aroused into wakefulness by my metronomic joint. I didn't get a call from the hospital until a little before six. I got there as they were wheeling him down a long, polished corridor. I was already way off in the deep end and I broke down next to a small shiny silver wheel while the procession was waiting for an elevator. Somebody white-coated and very kind helped me up off the ground and led me into a room with a TV. The man gave me a Coca-Cola that I tried to drink. Otherwise I floundered around for a good half hour, bumping into chairs and the floor while sobbing and moaning uncontrollably. The guy who makes you only dies once.

Eventually I came around.

I didn't see my father again until the morgue yesterday. He looked all right, a little pinker and puffier than usual. Then they closed the lid.

The funeral is set for three o'clock this afternoon. The day before my father "went" (he must have known he was "going") he had asked a nurse for a piece of paper and pen and wrote the following:

Adam my boy, since you're probably going to get stuck with getting rid of me, see if you can do me a couple of last favors. First, if possible, don't let anybody say anything at my funeral, especially anybody wearing a robe and/or a cross. All I want is music. Start with the last five minutes of The Marriage of Figaro. After that play Louis Armstrong's What a Wonderful World. Then play Willie Nelson's version of the same song. Sock it to 'em, baby. After Willie and Louis, if anybody still cares, finish with the last movement of Tchaikovsky's Sixth Symphony. Wolfgang Amadeus will make people feel good, Armstrong and Nelson will probably make them cry, and Tchaikovsky – with that last cello note drifting into nothingness – will give them a sense of who they are, i.e. crushed peanuts in the great Snickers in the sky. Maybe that's why he called it the "Pathétique". The whole thing should take less than thirty minutes. Anyway, I want no mention of the words God, heaven, resurrection, (I wouldn't have minded the word "erection" but fat chance anybody would say that at a funeral...haha) love, sin, savior, soul, or Jesus, or any of that kind of crap. Thanks kid. Try to honor your old man's last cerebral desire. Also, when they stick me in the ground don't let anybody sprinkle water or throw any flowers on me. It would be a waste of both. Adam, I love you like butterflies love the sun. All the best,

Your father,

Charley Lamb

Fortunately my girlfriend took care of most of the arrangements. I told her to try to get the little church in the vineyards in Mont-sur-Rolle. (My father used to say that he liked Swiss white wine "almost as much as the smell of pooh-pooh.") She reserved the building for us, then contacted the local pastor and made a deal that he could wear his outfit, but couldn't talk or throw any water. The local newspaper, 24 Heures, has a couple pages every day for dead people and funeral announcements, so my girlfriend had no trouble taking care of that. Hopefully whoever might want to show up will know about it.

The whole thing has been easier than I thought it would be. At least my girlfriend doesn't seem too stressed. In fact, she's handled everything with such ease that I wonder if my father hadn't primed her ahead of time. Which also makes me wonder if he hadn't had his nose in her fishbowl somewhere down the line. Actually, there probably won't be but a carload of people there anyway because Dad's list of friends had greatly diminished thanks to death or estrangement or both. The older he got the more people thought he was nuts. His wine seller, Jacques Bolle, should be there, and so should a few of his old girlfriends. But then again, most of them never quite figured out where he was coming from or going to. He used to tell them that he respected prostitutes more than he respected all presidents' wives going back to Eisenhower. He said perhaps both groups understood the nuts and bolts of life, but the former helped more people. Some newspaper people might show up, too. He wrote a weekly column in the sports page of the Lausanne tabloid for thirty years. In his last one a year ago he said, "Ninety-seven percent of everything in print is donkey crap," or some such thing.

This morning I was able to function, so I helped round up the music he asked for and my girlfriend made sure the sound system in the church was operational. We also reserved a big table at a café near the cemetery for a post-ceremony meal. So, I guess we're more or less ready to roll Dad into his last abode and to do it pretty close to how he wanted things. I hope a couple of his female friends show up. Or at least the nurse he tried to molest in the Morges hospital about ten days ago. The last time I went to visit him, the nurse, an adorable young Swiss-French woman with a Louise Brooks haircut that went perfectly with her charcoal eyes, told me he had placidly pawed her chest as she was escorting him to the toilet one night. She didn't seem too upset, but said it was against hospital regulations to have physical contact outside of the medical realm. She asked me if I'd inform him as such, which I did, to which he responded, "Screw the regulations and the little cutie pie."

Which reminds me of my morning stiffies. Which reminds me of how poor the English language is. We really only have a couple of words for the multifarious states of male excitation. We've got the standard medical term that Dad used in his last letter, i.e. "erection", the traditional locker-room "hard-on", and my gentler appellation, "stiffy". Other than that there's not much. How many words do the Eskimos have for the color of snow? I've heard they have a couple dozen. Well, shouldn't we be as creative with the masculine bulge? Here are a few possibilities that – for whatever reason – just popped into the old noggin:

1) Wet Noodle or Soft On: the floppy rubbery stiffy with weak intent.

2) Black & Decker: the steel stiffy that you think you could drill a hole in the wall with. (Hey man. I woke up with a Black and Decker and my wife ran upstairs and hid in the kids' bathroom...Yuk, yuk.)

3) Sleeping Beauty: the 4:20am wake-up stiffy that slowly but surely melts like an ice cream cone on a summer sidewalk.

4) Peter Pan or Pistillate Pencil: the mini-stiffy

that's attached to an eight or nine-year old body that has no idea what it's doing down there.

5) Eiffel Tower (my father's idea): the grandpa stiffy that stays hard for an hour or so until some soft hired hand takes it out of its misery and into the kingdom of geriatric relief.

6) Saturday Night Special: the married man stiffy that works quite like the clock on the wall, to wit, with undisturbed precision and monotony.

7) Pre-emptive Strike: the first date rocket that goes off after a hot kiss.

8) Pickled Pecker: the sloppy-drunk stiffy that, hard as it may try, embarrasses its owner as it rises to a feeble half of its potential grandeur.

9) Chili Dog: the stiffy that is so blood-filled that it burns at the head.

10) Oval Office: the stiffy attached to the fifty-five-year-old president or executive in a soft swivel chair that's begging for a secretary or an intern.

Well, so much for philology. I'm sure there could be lots more, but I need to start getting showered and dressed for Dad's funeral. As you can tell, I'm ready for it now. Yes, I was a basket case those first two days.

Cosmological orphanage hit hard. But now I'm pumped up. I've polished my shoes and thrown away the Kleenex box. I've cursed the black silence of the bottomless pit and wouldn't miss Dad's last public hurrah for a million bucks. I get it: life is a bitch. Losing the man who raised me was the last straw.

2

Excluding the pastor and the two gentlemen from the funeral parlor, there were twelve people in the church: my girlfriend and I, Mr. Bolle (the wine guy), his wife, the sports editor from the newspaper named Peter Pittet, his chunky foxy secretary, an old (in both time and space) American ex-patriot buddy of Dad's whom he called "Danny Dapper" and who is patiently waiting his turn to find out what happens when the lights really go out, and five women my father had played with over the last couple of decades, including the lovely nurse at the Morges hospital, very likely the last female he tried to get his hands on. He must have made some kind of impression on her given that she can't be a day over thirty (dear ol' Dad was seventy-one) and probably has rooms-full of dying patients. I say "get his hands on" not out of disrespect for women, but out of respect for Dad. Not too long ago he swore to me that when he hit fifty-five and finally closed out his last divorce, he would never get mad at a woman again, that women were his gods (goddesses) and, from then on, he would consider them all as coming from the toy store. They were there to have fun with…to enjoy life with! He said he didn't want to hear any of that pseudo-intellectual garbage about "femme objet", because no matter how hard our little brains shake and dance, the universe is always and forever "our object". The outside can never be the inside and vice-versa. Consciousness is always conscious "of" something, and after that "of" is an object. "Just because I wanna screw 'em," he said, "doesn't mean I don't respect 'em. Hell yes, I respect 'em – more than heaven can know. But I still wanna screw 'em." Women were Dad's gods in the eternal playground of his universe. Should he have been considered an asshole? You tell me…

In any case, Dad chose a beautiful day for his last rites: October 10th, a veiled sun blazing on the yellowing vineyards, a windless sixty degrees, and Mont Blanc and the other neighborly Alps pasted to the sky across Lake Geneva like pin-ups on Hugh Hefner's wall. On days like this, he used to say, "Heaven and earth are synonyms".

The ceremony was for three o'clock. My girlfriend and I left our apartment at one-thirty. She was wearing a beige summer dress and had a maroon shawl around her lovely shoulders. It looked like my father had chosen her clothes – she looked as sexy as she ever has and we were going to a funeral. I wore my only sport coat, a brown camel-hair thing that goes back about twenty years, but which looked great against the autumn vineyards (so one of my father's playmates said). I left out the tie because Dad never wore one. He said ties were just phony tails on the wrong side of the body, so what was the point? I went with a fancy black t-shirt, fashionable with actors and sports stars in the 1990s.

My girlfriend drove her little purple Toyota and I got to look out of the window at the Swiss version of Napa Valley, "La Côte". We exited the freeway in Rolle and as we headed up the road into the vineyards, I noticed the grapes had all been picked and the leaves were lucent. We were at the church by two, an hour before game time. The door was open and the coffin was inside angled like an arrow toward the audience.

There was a wreath of chrysanthemums (from whom I didn't know) on the coffin and a bouquet of yellow roses on a table next to it. Nobody was around. The funeral parlor guys were probably up at the café having a little of the region's famous white wine. Their silver and black body-mobile was parked next to the side door, but they were nowhere to be seen. I thought, *Hell, what if somebody had wanted to steal Dad...* I mean not him, but his last portable home. They run a few thousand francs and these days you never know what people will pilfer...

My girlfriend and I went back outside and sat down in the sun on a bench facing the lake. "How do you feel?" she asked.

"Like a ghost," I said.

"What do you mean?"

"I mean, we're all here today, gone tomorrow."

"And...?"

"And the living, in a sense, are already the dead. A week ago he was fondling nurses and now he's lying like a frozen tamale in that ugly copper crate in there."

She touched my hand and said, "It's a beautiful day."

"I know. He'd want us to make the best of it." I suddenly started to cry. I had thought I was cried out, emotionally squeezed dry, no more juice in the lemon.

But no, my eyes dripped until I heard some feet shuffling through the gravel behind us. "Somebody's coming," she said.

"It's either Zorro in white or the two vultures," I said trying to slow down the tears.

It was the vultures. They shuffled up to us red-cheeked looking like upright baby whales, "Bonjour…Bonjour," they said like robotic twins.

"Bonjour," my girlfriend responded.

"Toute est en ordre," the older one offered.

"Il fait beau," chirped his partner.

"Oui, oui," my girlfriend added.

We followed them into the building, for what reason I didn't know. It was still forty-five minutes before the funeral. I had forgotten a handkerchief so I dried my eyes and face with my coat sleeve. They showed us the coffin and said they had ordered the flowers themselves because they hadn't received any from anybody else. I told them Dad had wanted a flowerless funeral since he thought his own death was enough, and there was no sense in adding innocent flora to the baleful mix. I nearly offered to pay for them, but figured they'd simply be added to the bill. They asked how many people we were expecting, pointing out that the church could only hold about a hundred. I assured them space wouldn't be a problem.

My girlfriend and I then went back outside to the bench.

At two-thirty the pastor's feet stirred the gravel. He looked like he had just awakened from a nap. The fact that he didn't have to say anything at the service probably allowed him an afternoon snooze, which he otherwise might not have had time for. Then again, maybe he always gives pretty much the same speech and so doesn't have too much to prepare. But what did I know? He had his outfit on. Like I said, Zorro in white without the mask. He was even sporting the mini-sombrero. He shook our hands, two of his for one of ours. He cupped mine like it was some kind of dying bird. He asked me if I was who he imagined me to be, i.e. the son of the deceased. I confirmed I was, to which he said, "Je vois, mon fils." He finally let go of my hand and smiling at my girlfriend said, "Madame has informed me of your desire to have a funeral with only music." I told him it was Dad's idea, not mine. He said he would respect our wish as much as possible. I didn't push him on what that meant. To be honest, he did seem like a rather decent guy.

At a quarter to three Jacques Bolle and his wife showed up, nodding hello and then slipping discreetly into the church. A couple minutes later Peter Pittet, the newspaperman, and his girlfriend strolled in. She must have carried a hundred and eighty pounds on her five-foot-six frame, but nonetheless bared as much of it as she could under the early autumn circumstances. She had on a short black skirt, a thin red jacket, and a V-neck pale pink blouse that had trouble dealing with the size of her enormous breasts. Pittet had his arm around her invisible waist as they crossed the yard to greet us. He was a thin man of about sixty with a chiseled face whose principal diet – so my father had told me – was Gitane cigarettes and Pastis. My father had liked him and had often told me stories they had shared at the newspaper bar. The one I remember most clearly was about an elderly (late seventies) male friend whom Pittet met every morning around eleven for an aperitif in the Café Lorado across the street from the newspaper building. The man had been depressed because he couldn't get it up anymore. "It's the only thing I have left," he told Pittet, "and it's dead. I try and I try and I can't." Pittet didn't see him for a couple of weeks and thought maybe the man was dead. Finally he showed up one morning with an ear-to-ear smile, "I tried and I tried and I could," he said, and bought everybody in the place a drink.

The four of us went into the church a few minutes before three. The clergyman had removed his wide brim and was standing next to the coffin in a pose not unlike that of a bodyguard. My girlfriend was doing the music, so she went to ask him when we should get started. He gestured toward the barren church, looked at his watch, then whispered something to her. She came back to me and said we should wait a few more minutes, at least until the church bell struck thrice. I whispered to her that maybe Dad's old girlfriends were waiting until the last second such that they could slip in unnoticed, like politicians into titty bars. Just then the nurse walked in and seeing her out of uniform I understood why Dad had tried to fondle her. If they have funeral magazines, she should be on the cover of next month's edition. She smiled at us and like a swan landing on the lake, gently floated onto a bench at the back.

The bell dinged, danged, and donged and my girlfriend went to the music set-up off to the side behind the coffin. The pastor wanted to say something, I could tell, but just smiled and held his tongue, then sat down next to the pulpit. My eyes met my girlfriend's, I nodded, and the music started…the end of The Marriage of Figaro. It was an old recording with Guiseppe Di Stephano and Anna Moffo that my father had played probably more than any other music he had. He used to say, "It's the one piece of music that makes me believe there might be a God…and if there is, his name is Mozart". My throat thickened and to distract myself I turned sideways and glanced back toward the nurse and the door. A woman walked in.

Then another...and another...and another. Dad still had friends.

It was Louis Armstrong's turn. He saw fields of green. Red roses, too. So did Willie Nelson. Then my girlfriend played the last movement of Tchaikovsky's Sixth. I don't know what it did for everybody else, but on me it had the effect my father had hoped for. The last note died and I was sawdust…Then the pastor stood up and went to the microphone.

I should have known he couldn't get through a whole ceremony without talking. He thanked my girlfriend for the beautiful music, checked his notes, and proceeded to say that Charles Bryce Lamb had led a wonderful life and where he was now was even more wonderful. I looked at him, but he was staring straight ahead above the heads of the angels in the back pews. He was only doing his job, keeping sure the world knew that God somehow had everything under control. He couldn't have babbled for more that five minutes, so what could I say? It was probably a record for the shortest funeral speech by a man in a long robe.

Dad was dead. The funeral was over. We all followed the hearse up the street to the cemetery and laid him in the ground. The pastor held his tongue. The silence was golden and all eyes were misty except the globes under the white sombrero. He'd done this too often to cry. And besides, when you believe God is there to clean up each and every mess, there isn't much left to shed a tear for.

3

Everyone (except the pastor and the vultures – had they flown off to another corpse?) followed my girlfriend and me to the café. As we stood mingling, I asked everybody if white wine was okay to drink as a last hommage to my father's predilection for the Féchys, Mont-sur-Rolles, and Luins that had filled his gut since he discovered them forty-five years prior. Only Jacques Bolle's wife wanted mineral water. The waitress laid out the glasses, bottles arrived, glasses were filled, and I raised mine to thank everybody for their presence. Then Peter Pittet took the floor and proposed a toast, "Here's to Charley Lamb, one of finest animals ever to roam the earth. He was a buffalo, a lion, a rabbit, and a kitten all rolled into one. He ate the world, drank the world, licked the world, and made love to the world. May we love him forever.… Santé everybody!"

The chasselas went down smoothly. There was a silent moment until Danny Dapper spoke up, loud enough for everyone to hear. "Adam, that was my kind of ceremony. If the music was your idea, you should patent it. And for once, the gentleman in the white robe stayed out of it for the most part and let it be Charley's moment. It was a great funeral in a wonderful world." Dapper raised his glass for a second toast.

Eventually everybody took a seat at a big rectangular wooden table. I was at the end with my girlfriend on my left. Danny Dapper squeezed in between her and the nurse. To my right was a woman I didn't know of about forty-five with an Eastern European accent, hair in a disheveled ponytail, a well-shaped nose and yellow-brown eyes. She said she was from Romania. When I asked her what she did in life, she said she was a singer. I wondered how my father had met her, how long they had known each other, and what they had done together. (I later found out, more or less.) Pittet was across from Dapper between the Romanian and his secretary. Next to her was the tall young woman who had been the last person to enter the church. I remember thinking she looked like a famous TV weatherwoman or a high-priced whore, or both. In any case, she seemed happy to be in the group and laughed at most everything said, especially Pittet's wisecracks. I think she was Swiss as she had no perceptible accent. She was the first person to call the waitress over for a second helping of wine. I overheard her tell Pittet – over his secretary's shoulder – that parties after funerals were often the best parties of all because everybody was so relaxed after such a spill of emotion. Had my father been there, I imagined he'd have been sitting in the empty chair next to her. He was a master at sniffing out the tiniest sign of a woman in heat. After a short conversation with the Romanian, I went over and introduced myself. Her name was Barbara Chardon.

"Did you know my father well?" I asked

"I used to read his stuff in the newspaper. Actually the first time I ever really met him was at a get-together like this after my uncle died."

"Well, it was nice of you to come," I said.

"Charley told me a lot about you, Adam."

"Had you known him long?" My curiosity was rising.

"Let's see," she said rolling her eyes. "We must have

met three or four years ago. When did he stop writing in the paper?"

"Just last year."

"Yes, my uncle's been dead for at least three years."

"How did my father know your uncle?"

"He worked at the newspaper too. His funeral was up in Grandvaux. I remember it like yesterday. The post-funeral party was in that famous restaurant that overlooks the lake and everything, in the middle of those huge vineyards." She waved a finger toward the east. "It was a beautiful day just like today. But it was in the spring I think...April. Yeah, I'm sure it was. Charley and I were the last ones to leave the restaurant. He offered to give me a ride home."

What a guy, I thought. "That was nice of him," I said.

"He was one of the most interesting people I've ever known. He was different. He didn't care about stuff other people cared about and what he cared about other people didn't."

"Yeah, I know what you mean."

Peter Pittet had been talking to the Romanian singer. Suddenly he tuned into our conversation. "I heard you say something about your uncle," he said across his secretary to Barbara Chardon.

"We were talking about how I met Charley. It was

at my uncle's funeral."

"Yes, a lucky day for everybody," he said winking at me. "Adam, I knew Barbara long before Charley did. Her uncle wrote for the paper for thirty years. We were very close too."

His secretary caustically asked if he wanted to change places. He brushed her off and said, "Barbara, which piece of the music Adam chose reminded you the most of Charley?"

So the shark must have known her well, I thought.

"They all did," she said. "But the Louis Armstrong one got me the most because the last time I was with Charley in France, he played it in the car a couple of times. He said the world really was a wonderful place and if you looked around, there was far more beauty than ugliness."

The lucky son of a bitch! France? In the car?

"Where did you and my father go in France?" I asked.

"Oh, he took me to a nice restaurant in Alsace. Ill...Ill...Ill*house* something. The food was superb." She looked at her empty glass. Pittet called the waitress. As she filled the glasses, he turned back to the Romanian woman and I told Barbara how nice it was to have met her and I got up and moved on around the table to my father's friend, Jacques Bolle, and his wife. They thanked me for the aperitif, but said they had to be going soon. I hoped the others stuck around for a while.

Next to them was another woman I didn't know who was probably a few days into her late fifties. I had noticed that she didn't seem to care who she was talking to or about what. She had a natural contented grin that made her thin lips look thicker than they were. Her hair was short and grey-black. She comfortably wore a black dress that seemed to have been designed to let us know she had a comely cleavage. A cute slightly beaked nose lived under almond eyes. It was apparent she had been rather beautiful in her younger days. My guess was she had known my father long ago.

"I'm Adam," I said.

"And I'm Louise, but your father called me Lou-Lou. Actually I knew him long before you did."

"I thought you might have," I said not surprised.

"As far as I know, I was his first girlfriend in Switzerland. I met him shortly after he got here. He was giving English lessons in a school I went to."

"I didn't know that," I offered not knowing he had ever taught his native language.

"He didn't stay in the school too long. Just long enough for us to fall in love. As soon as he left the school we became intimate. I think he was about twenty-six and I was seventeen."

The rascal, I thought. "How long were you together?"

"Pretty close to three years…"

"Really?"

"Yes…He had a little Volkswagen beetle and we traveled all over southern Europe every chance we got. Mostly Italy and France. We didn't have a lot of money, but we didn't need much." She chuckled and delicately lifted her glass to her lips. "Adam," she said, "Charley was one of the few men I've known who knew where the bottom of the barrel was…or maybe I should say, who knew the barrel of life was bottomless."

"Yeah, I guess so," I said not really sure what she meant.

"We would eat, drink, and make love anywhere and everywhere."

At the time this woman – girl – wasn't even old enough to get a driver's license, I thought. *The bastard! Haha! Dear ol' Dad.* It was kind of too bad we hadn't had this funeral before he died. I would have liked to ask him a few things about what I was learning. "Had you seen him recently?" I asked.

"No, not for years. I've lived in Paris for a long

time. I happened to be here for another funeral two days ago and I saw in the paper that he had died. This is my second funeral in three days."

"I'm sorry."

"Don't be. We all die. I enjoyed this one. Thanks. You did a good job, Adam."

"It was all Dad," I said. "I mean it was all his idea."

"I kind of thought so."

"Yeah, he left me a note in the hospital the night before he died."

"Good for him. He used to listen to some of that music when I knew him. I guess some things don't change."

"Could be," I said, trying to imagine this woman forty years ago. Then I looked at the nurse three chairs away that had politely resisted Dad's roaming hand a couple weeks back, but who had liked him enough to come to his funeral. Who knows? Maybe, she had let the old codger have a little.

"How did he die, if I might ask?" Louise said pointing her eyes at mine.

"He had a lung problem. But he had had it for years. He refused to go to a doctor until it was way too late. That's what the hospital said anyway. He went pretty fast."

"Good," she said. "I hope I do, too. My mother

rotted for five years, turned into a vegetable, then rotted for five more. I'm sure Charley wouldn't have wanted to go that way. Where had he been living these past years?"

"In Tolochenaz, just outside of Morges. He had been there for about twenty years."

"That's where Audrey Hepburn is buried. He and I used to walk in the fields and vineyards behind the little cemetery sometimes. He always liked the area. One summer we had been winetasting in Denges and we walked down to Tolochenaz and he took a bath in the fountain in the middle of the village. He tried to pull me in with him. He looked for every excuse to put his paws on me," she said with a lovely grin.

"Doesn't surprise me," I said.

She suddenly turned pensive. I told her it was a pleasure to have met her and moved further along the table to say a few words to the nurse.

4

For some of us Charley Lamb's farewell party lasts longer than expected. Jacques Bolle and his wife leave at about five. At six, my girlfriend goes back to our house to feed the dogs. She says she might be back, but I doubt she will. The nurse leaves shortly after explaining that she has to work the night shift. Her departure seems to sadden all the men at the table. She dutifully gives everyone three kisses and even asks me if she can pay for anything. Whoever marries this angel won't regret it…

By seven everybody who has stayed is quite drunk and the alcohol in Pittet's secretary's head seems to suddenly sour her mood. She lets loose with a few invectives about her boss's flirtatious habits. He shoots back with a few gems of his own. Then she, with his subtle encouragement, takes the keys to his car, gets up from her chair like a whale from a sea, blandly pops Pittet across the side of his head with her handbag, and disappears into the starry October evening.

The quorum of twelve has now been reduced to six. I am back sitting next to my father's first Swiss girlfriend. The Romanian singer is next to her. Pittet is next to Barbara Chardon. Danny Dapper has moved in between Pittet and the Romanian. We are in kind of a semi-circle, down at my end of the long table. Lips are loosening and joy is returning as is wont to happen when death crashes into the world, looms, lingers, and pains, then slips out the back door leaving the living cathartically happy to be alive. Pittet is now doing everything in his power to keep Barbara Chardon in place; Danny Dapper is intently listening to the Romanian and feeling a resurrection of his aging loins; my father's first girlfriend, "Lou-Lou" as she calls herself, is twirling my head with stories about my maker and his first few years in his newly adopted country.

Pittet suggests we have a giant fondue. Everyone agrees. An excuse to order more wine.

Encore une, he mouths to the waitress as he holds up the empty bottle. She is back in a minute, uncorking the bottle and filling the glasses. Pittet then taps his glass with a knife, stands, and calls the group to order. "Ladies and gentlemen," he solemnly declares with his gravelly tobacco-stained voice, "Charley Lamb has brought us together and Charley Lamb has a few things he wants to say. So please listen while he speaks, one last time, to the lucky living." Pittet is visibly tipsy and in a jovial mood. He looks around the café to see if guests at other tables are listening. An elderly couple finishing a fondue lift their long forks in acknowledgement. Two young lovers sharing a dessert stop eating and tune in. Pittet has the floor and, imitating my father's thick American accent, begins his monologue: "O life…O beauty…O nonsense…Life's beauty is not in sense, but in nonsense. For thousands of years…since Plato and his fair friends roamed the streets of Athens…we…the people…have tried to make sense out of nonsense." He slightly totters and puts a hand on Barbara Chardon's shoulder. "Yes, we have created a slew of glorious gods. We have written lofty constitutions and made laws to keep the jungle as safe as possible. But under this façade of order and understanding, there is a glorious chaos. The real glory of the world is that it has no creator, no purpose, no reason to be. It simply is. Imagine the wonder and marvel of that. No god, no logic, no innate meaning or sense. What could be more beautiful than that? Only man tries to give life a higher purpose. Other animals don't do it. They just want to eat, procreate, live, and die. Stars and planets and moons don't do it. They are content to burn, rotate, and fly. But we humans want to give it all a grand logic and reason to be! We want more! We want truth, history, justice, equality, and love! We want a coherent story with a beginning and an end. We want creator and commandments…" Pittet pauses and sips his chasselas. He is obviously enjoying himself… "We are such greedy bastards! Why can't we just be satisfied with what we have…Life…A chance to live…A chance to be…to roam in the jungle with all the other glorious animals. Why do we always want more? But not I…not Charley Lamb. I have had a chance to live. That is enough. For let us remember that life is the exception, not the rule. Life! – a rare ray of light in a dark, vast, eternal cosmos. Imagine how far the stars are from each other. Imagine the vast nothingness…. Yes, we are the lucky ones, so lucky to have been and to be here together in this glorious café…celebrating my life, not crying over my death!" Pittet raises his glass. A few people clap. Some drink. He sits down.

The waitress places two flaming devices on the table and lights them. Within seconds the chef appears with a steaming pot of fondue in each hand.

5

"Here's one I've never forgotten," Danny Dapper says. "It must have been twenty years ago. Charley and I went into a big chic department store in Lausanne. He wanted to buy a present for his kid – yeah, you, Adam!... So we're looking for cologne or some such thing and as we walk toward the men's toiletries, we pass the women's toiletries, and we both see this gorgeous heavily made-up woman with a low cut blouse with lots of goodies inside. We both smile at her and she smiles back. We go buy the cologne and get it gift-wrapped. Then Charley says we need to go back and see that beautiful woman again. There she is behind her perfume counter. Charley slowly walks up real close to her, cranes his neck, and peeks down her blouse. 'May I help you!' she says stiffly as she backpedals a step or two. Now don't forget Charley's going on sixty and this woman is probably thirty-five. 'No thanks,' Charley says, 'I just wanted to have a look at your beautiful breasts.' The woman – who, of course, in another world could have been happy and taken Charley's actions as a compliment – is incensed and starts ranting and raving about what a pig Charley is. Charley stays totally calm and keeps gazing down her blouse. Finally she says she's going to call the manager or the police or National Guard or something. So Charley coolly backs away and says, 'Chère Madame, why do you wear a blouse like that if you don't want me to look down it?' Then we walked away and out the door."

"I've got one, too, of a different kind," Pittet says downing his shot of Kirsch, the post-fondue chaser. "Charley and I were going to play golf early one morning on this course up in the Jura mountains in France. It's foggy and cold and we're driving – he's driving – through this forest just before you get to the border. He suddenly sees a big snail in the middle of the road and swerves to avoid it. He goes another hundred meters or so, then turns the car around and goes back. Without saying a word, he stops the car, gets out, goes and picks up the snail and puts it in the grass on the other side of the road. When he gets back in the car, I say, 'Charley, you're one crazy SOB.' And he says, 'Not as crazy as that snail there…'"

Everybody is drunk, especially Barbara Chardon. She's laughing tears as the stories are told. When she finally calms down, she says. "One time…one time with me we were eating a sandwich down by the lake in Ouchy and all these little birds came around our feet. He took one bite of his sandwich, and then gave all the rest to the birds. When I asked him why, he said, 'I gave you one. I might as well give them one.'" She laughs again and downs the last drop of her Kirsch.

Pittet orders six more.

It's the Romanian singer's turn. Her name, we now know, is Isabella. She leans back and smiles at Barbara Chardon. "I've never told anybody this, but I met Charley in a night club, what the Swiss call 'a cabaret'. It's really just a glorified whorehouse, of course. It turns out that the only job I could get to get me out of Romania. The guy who hired me said I'd get a chance to use my voice. Fat chance! The only songs I could sing were to myself to the stupid disco music that played in the background all the time. Otherwise my job was to get men to buy me champagne. If they bought me a bottle, they could take me in the back and, one way or another, relieve themselves, if you know what I mean. Well, one night in Lausanne, here was this guy sitting alone at the bar watching the circus. He looked to be in no hurry for anything, so I went up to talk to him to try to get him to buy me a glass of champagne. I should add that I was near the end of my four-month contract and was less and less inclined to hustle the clients. But this guy looked interesting."

Here Pittet pipes up and says, "Honey, don't apologize. You were just doing Salvation Army work!" Even people at the next table laughed.

Isabella goes on. "So anyway, it was Charley, and he starts asking me questions about myself and he actually acted like he cared about me and my situation. I'll never forget one thing he said – that he respected us women who worked in these places more than all the presidents' wives in America. And he was dead serious. He told me I was doing mankind a great service, but he could understand how I'd rather sing. It turns out he invited me to dinner on my day off and after dinner he asked me to sing for him. He took me back to his apartment and I sang. Honestly, he was the first guy in Switzerland who made me feel like I was more than a piece of meat."

The Kirsches come. Pittet makes a wise crack about Charley getting his flute played, and then Isabella finishes her story.

"To make a long story short, when my four months were up, Charley helped me find a job teaching music in a school in Montreux and I was able to get a permit and stay in Switzerland. We kept in touch off and on for quite a few years. I always thought that with people like him in this country, it was a good place to be. And I've been here twenty-five years now."

I didn't know about the others, but I felt a few tears welling up. I mean this guy was my father! Lou-Lou noticed my damp eyes and whispered something to the effect that it was interesting what you find when you turn on the lights in the closet. What was also interesting was that as the evening wore on, all these people around the table, though at least a half a century old – except Barbara Chardon and myself – started looking much younger. I began seeing their faces as if they were the ages they were when all these things happened. Lou-Lou was seventeen. Isabella was twenty-five. Pittet and Danny Dapper were cruising through their forties and fifties. And I was seeing my father through the years after he moved to Switzerland and made a life for himself – both before and after he made me.

Peter Pittet had the last story… "You know, there weren't many people Charley really liked. He loved humanity in general, but he had trouble with it in particular. He often told me that the older he got, the more he thought human beings were such odd creatures. Like probably all of us here – except maybe you, Adam – Charley was raised a Christian, and good Christians are supposed to love all of God's children. When Charley stopped believing in the Christian God, he kind of stopped believing in God's children. People lost their sons-and-daughters-of-divinity status. They lost their credentials. They started looking like strange – very strange – creatures. We talked about this often these past few years. We'd be sitting in a café and he'd say, 'Look at that guy over there. Do you see a man? What is a man? I see as much a ghost as I do a man. I see an ethereal composition of lines, dots, and colors, but where is the core? Where is the center? What are we all really? Yeah, we call ourselves human beings, but what does that mean? The longer I live, the less I know for sure.' And then he would always add something like, 'Well, one thing is for damn sure…compared to cats, butterflies, and flowers, we really are kind of ugly…' Yeah, that was my friend Charley Lamb."

6

It was close to midnight when we started stirring to leave the café. The waitress had put the chairs on the other tables and was sweeping the place clean. I called her over for the bill. Danny Dapper wanted to pay. Pittet fumbled through his clothes for his wallet. But this was Charley Lamb's party and Charley Lamb had left his son plenty of money to foot the bill. As we walked outside everybody was more or less holding on to each other. I think the only one who was reasonably sober was Lou-Lou. I thought about going back inside and ordering a couple of taxis to make sure everybody got home alive. But the night air hit me and I decided not to. Everybody had a car except Pittet. I offered to take him home, but evidently he had already worked out transportation with Barbara Chardon. We all hugged, three-kissed, and said goodbye. I lingered a bit looking out over the lake at the twinkle of lights in Evian and Thonon-les-Bains. The moon hung like a streetlamp over the Alps. As I was ambling toward my car, there were soft footsteps behind me and I felt a hand touch my elbow. It was Lou-Lou. "Come on," she said softly, "let's go say hello to Charley."

She held my arm and we walked back to the cemetery. The gate squeaked. The light bouncing off the moon was sufficient such that we could see the names of the dead and know their years of living. We went to where Dad was, the hole freshly covered with dark earth.

"I loved him," she said. "And so did your mother." She rose on her toes and kissed the side of my neck.

PART II

<h1 style="text-align:center">7</h1>

The town of Morges, where my girlfriend and I live, is cut in half by the freeway. The story goes that when they built Switzerland's first freeway in 1964, the A1 from Geneva to Lausanne, the mayor of Morges had a house in an unpopulated area that was right next to where the highway was supposed to pass, a couple of miles west of the town center. He evidently finagled things such that the four-lane road was re-routed and ended up cutting right through one of the more populated parts of the city. Anyway – to sprint to the point – property values next to the freeway are naturally peanuts compared to the rest of the beautiful town. There is a thin strip of land smack dab between the train tracks and the freeway. Three houses had been in the middle of the planned freeway. Instead of being destroyed, they were actually picked up and moved two hundred meters to this blessed promised land! This is where my girlfriend and I live. I bought the house three years ago for less than half the price of what it would have been were it situated a stone's throw to the east or west. Like they say in real estate, "Location is everything". I got a great house dirt-cheap! The agent who sold it to me told me that he got hundreds of calls for the place because it was so cheap. But so as to not waste time, he would be up front with everybody and immediately tell them where it was situated. He said only three people ever came and looked at it, and I was the only one who said the location was no problem at all! And we love the place. It has a nice grassy garden with a big beautiful blue pine in the middle and a fence all around to keep our animals off the highway and train tracks. There are cute little patches of flowers that show up every spring through no doing of ours. We have two dogs, two attics, two garages, and plenty of rooms to stay out of each other's way. My girlfriend has a sewing room, I have a room to work and listen to music in, and there are two extra rooms upstairs. My father always told me that if you look around the world, you see that we human beings can adapt to pretty much anything and everything. He was right: after a week we stopped hearing the trains and the cars. I tell my friends, "Hell, people pay fortunes to live in New York or Paris or Tokyo. What's wrong with a little noise? And if you listen to the drone of the freeway with an open mind, it sounds just like the ocean."

The two attics are coming in handy. For the past month I've been going through Dad's stuff and am having a hard time throwing it away. What do you do? You're Adam Lamb, forty years old, no brothers or sisters, no descendants; you haven't had a mother since you can remember. All you've got is a girlfriend, dogs, a house, and a car. Your father dies. You don't throw his life away. You put it in your attic, box after box of it. That line of boxes is your umbilical cord. It's all you've got left to tie your story to the earth.

Right now there are a dozen Chiquita banana boxes on the floor in the smaller attic next to the bathroom. This attic had been empty except for two rolled rugs the dogs had pissed on multiple times. I've been combing through Dad's stuff like a mother monkey inspecting her baby's head for fleas. I've read all kinds of things and dissected a drawer-full of photographs, mostly of women, some clad, some not. Not surprisingly, there was a hearty collection of Barbara

Chardon looking like she was advertising underwear. I suspect her body was Dad's idea of perfection. He had it in Technicolor and in black and white from all angles. Isabella, the Romanian, was in that drawer too a few times. She, however, was always clothed, and most of the photos were close-ups of her face. It must have been those amber "animal" eyes. And then there was a very young woman, often in a loose white cotton robe, with short cropped hair, a swan's neck, and dark eyes seated next to canals and statues and on boardwalks and terraces in various Italian and French cities – Siena, Pisa, Rome, San Remo, Nice, Avignon, Arles, and Paris. These were at the bottom of the drawer. Only the locations were noted on the backs of some of them. No names. I wondered if the woman might have been Lou-Lou. There were other women, too, and a few pictures of my father spanning decades – a decked-out cowboy riding a fold-up bed, a smiling kid in a baggy baseball suit or with a yo-yo trophy, a skinny teenager in a basketball uniform, one in his twenties where he had a moustache and long curly hair standing next to a Navajo woman in Monument Valley, others on the lip of the Grand Canyon, in a café in Venice, skiing in Davos, hiking in the Jungfrau…. Yes, the ol' man lived before he died.

I was in a few pictures, mostly as a baby in a

highchair or a playpen staring big-eyed at the camera. I was always with my father or alone, except for one picture where we see my tiny face, probably a month old, and the back of a woman's head.

Of course I've been looking for clues about my mother…for about thirty years now. But all the windows and mirrors are frosted. In any case, does one really miss what one has never had? All I know is a conversation I had with my father that happened on my tenth birthday. I distinctly remember that I had a party with my friends in the afternoon and that night he took me to McDonald's. Sitting together in a corner booth, I asked him about "my mom". He said that she was a wonderful woman who left our world shortly after I was born and that before she left she told her son (me) every day that she loved him more than anything else in the world. That was all Charley Lamb said, no more, no less. I remember the moment like it was last week. A few years later – I must have been sixteen or seventeen – I asked him about her again and he said that I already knew all there was to know. He repeated what he had said about her leaving our world and loving me. Then he did something I had never seen him do before; he started to cry. Without another word he left the room and the house. I recall going to the window and seeing him in his car with his head and hands on the steering wheel. He stayed like that for what must have been five minutes, and then he drove away. He didn't come back until the next morning. I guess seeing him like that is why I never asked him about my mother again.

As you can imagine, Charley Lamb was a wonderful father. I never remember him yelling at me or spanking me. I just remember the fun. As I was growing up he used to often say that he couldn't get mad at a cloud so how could he get pissed off at me. In a sense, it was a privileged father-son relationship because he had only me and I had only him. There was no third person to pull on the strings and mess with the mix. We took walks together, skied together, shopped together, cleaned house together. He took me with him to New York, San Francisco, Rome, and Madrid, to operas, concerts, sporting events, and movies. But it was always just the two of us. He never brought any of his girlfriends.

We lived alone together in Lausanne until I went off to the university in Arizona. He had always wanted me to have a few years of "the American experience". While I was gone he married a woman, divorced, quickly wed another, then threw in the towel. I knew neither of his wives well, just seeing them at Christmas and a bit in the summer. After he divorced the first one, I'll never forget what he said about her… "She thought there was no difference between my prick and a dildo. To which I responded, 'There probably isn't except that one works best for me and the other works best for you.'" As the for second wife, one summer on the balcony after a little too much wine, he offered this insight: "She married me then decided to become a member of the movement for the liberation of the female. I told her the only liberated women were either dead or on the waiting list to be born." Of course he thought the same thing about men. He used to say, "We're all free to be somebody's slave," meaning the idea of freedom looked great on paper and in political speeches, but if you really thought about it, it was a rather foggy notion that resembled clouds more than concrete. He and that second wife stayed together a year, which he said was perfect because "She had just enough time to teach me everything I didn't need to know."

He had left Lausanne and moved into the apartment in Tolochenaz with this second wife because she supposedly "wanted to be closer to nature". My father firmly believed that everything in existence was nature (and that man and everything man-made was part of it), but he also believed in trying to be a nice guy, so he agreed to make the change thinking it might save an unraveling marriage. It didn't work, but after she moved out, he never left Tolochenaz. He stayed there for twenty years, until the day he checked into the Morges hospital, which he affectionately called, "my last cradle". Dad thought the world was home; he tried to make things cozy wherever he was.

I'm almost finished sorting through all his stuff. It really is hard to toss any of the last remnants of the man that was Charley Lamb into the trashcan. My guess is that I'll fill up another three or four Chiquita banana boxes. From then on Charley will live in my attic. I can't help wondering what will remain of him after I'm gone. If I have a kid, he or she will never know him. How much can you care about somebody you've never met?

For some reason, I always come alone to his apartment in Tolochenaz. My girlfriend has offered to help many times, but I always refuse her offer. I guess it's because I want the two of us – father and son – to be together one last time.

Recently I finished reading his old newspaper columns. He had cut them out and saved them in the bottom desk drawer. I think the one that struck me most was about the soccer coach of the English national team, Glenn Hoddle, who got fired because he said handicapped people were handicapped because they were paying for sins committed in a prior life. Without my father's permission, I print what he had to say:

THE GLENN HODDLE AFFAIR

"Public opinion exists, only where there are no ideas."
Oscar Wilde

GLENN HODDLE WAS RECENTLY SWEPT AWAY as coach of the English National Team. The public and the press held the broom.

Hoddle believes in reincarnation. He believes, therefore, that we live life after life in different bodies and as different creatures. He is not alone in this belief. Whole civilizations in the Orient share his conviction. Hoddle told somebody (a journalist, I think) that he believed people who are handicapped in this world are so because they are paying for some bad behavior in a previous life. For this statement the politically correct European presses started shouting "scandal" and within a few days, Hoddle was fried chicken.

In no way do I share Hoddle's belief in either reincarnation or his theory as to why people are handicapped. But I want to ask a question that I haven't heard anyone else ask: "How different are Hoddle's beliefs from another religious conviction that claims that people who do bad things in this life will be punished—in hell or otherwise—in the next life?"

The prominent religion of the Western Hemisphere often tells people that if they sin too much during their earthly sojourn, they will suffer for it after death. This notion ("hell") has been toned down some in recent decades, but it is still a belief that I'm sure many football coaches hold today. Is this belief really very different from Mr. Hoddle's? Is it not essentially the same concept only in a different temporal order? Hoddle claims people are paying now. The other concept says people will pay later. But coaches who are part of this religion are never burned at the stake for such a belief. Why? Because their belief is part of one tradition and Mr. Hoddle's is part of another tradition.

The moral of the story is that straying from one's tradition is often badly viewed by the public. And the public has a tendency to howl before it thinks, if, that is, it ever thinks at all.

This Hoddle business reminded me of what Barbara Chardon said about my father caring about things that other people didn't care about. Here's one of his articles that made me think of Peter Pittet's speech in the restaurant and how Charley Lamb liked fewer and fewer people the longer he lived:

WHERE HAVE YOU GONE JOE DIMAGGIO?

"To say that man is an animal flatters man."

I AM NOT PROUD TO BE a human these days. Monica Lewinsky is making sure.

Of course it is not Monica's fault. She is, in no way, the cause. It is the people of the world who are fueling my shame.

Monica, as far as I can tell, is a most ordinary person. She has no quality, nor has said one thing, nor has done one act, that merits any special attention. And yet she consumes the interest of humanity. Humanity is such a sad species.

Humanity may or may not have always been a sad species. I wasn't there in the past and I won't be there for much longer in the future. But what I am witnessing in my lifetime is a sorry spectacle.

But Monica is only part of a big flood. Most of what I see in music and cinema reminds me of Monica, i.e. mediocrity or worse. I went to see two films that have been nominated for this year's Oscar award for Best Picture. Excessive violence had me walking out of both after a half an hour. I recently tried to watch MTV; it made me think about what Dante's Inferno must be really like.

But music and cinema are only part of a big flood. Much of what I see in sports reminds me of music and cinema. Today's athletes, most of whom are very mediocre people, get treated like gods. They in turn treat the world like a cheap motel.

There is no substance to so much of what we see in sports, music, cinema, and Monica. There is surface: glitter and money and scandal. The characters are all interchangeable. They are fast-food facades that fill the empty stomach of a humanity that has nothing inside.

People today don't see respect and work and honorable behavior. They don't see beauty. They don't want work, honorable behavior, beauty and respect for life. They want Monica. They want vacuous fast food.

Example: Americans today know far more about

President Clinton's sexual activities that his political activities. Much more.

Example: Sports pages have ten times more stories about scandal and drugs and cheating than about honorable athletes. Mike Tyson, steroids, misused Olympic cash...this is the fools' fodder.

Example: Joe DiMaggio just died. He was a baseball hero fifty years ago. The hero. He was a great man. He valued himself. Not as a celebrity, but as a man. He respected others. Someone once asked him toward the end of his career, why he still worked so hard when he had nothing left to prove. "Because," he said calmly, "there might be some young boy watching who has never seen me play before." Are there any Joe DiMaggios out there today?

In this year of 1999, we have so many telephones, so many TV stations, so much www.com, so much music, so much press, so much cinema, but...but is anybody saying anything?

Paul Simon wrote a song in the Sixties in which he asked, "Where have you gone Joe DiMaggio?" Answer: You have been replaced by Monicas.

The question is often asked if animals have souls. It is not animals we should be wondering about.

My father used to say his early love for sports was like

the love a boy has for the smell of fresh cookies in the kitchen.

WILT

NEWSPAPERS LIE. TELEVISIONS LIE. RADIOS LIE. Magazines lie. Let's just say the media lie.

On October 14, 1999 they all announced the death of Wilt Chamberlain at age 63. But Wilt Chamberlain isn't dead. I have proof.

I know a boy who lies in his bed in the suburbs of San Francisco with a transistor radio tucked against his ear. He is supposed to be asleep, but he is listening to play-by-play of the San Francisco Warriors against the Los Angeles Lakers.

... Pass to Chamberlain ... he spins in the key ... the Dipper Dunk ...TWO!! ... That's forty-five for Wilt ... Goodrich drives ... shoots ... Blocked by Wilt ... Guy Rodgers picks up the loose ball ... passes to Mechery ... inside to Wilt ... make that forty-seven for Wilt! ...Warriors 95 - Lakers 89 with four minutes to go ...

Wilt will score fifty-three points and the Warriors

will win. The boy in his bed will count every point and know the score at every moment. He will turn off the radio after the last post-game interview. He will be tired tomorrow at school, but it doesn't matter. The Warriors have won. Wilt has scored fifty-three, grabbed twenty-two rebounds and blocked six shots. It is 1962.

It is 1999. Wilt still floats through the boy's cerebral radio. Call the boy a man if you want to, but that would probably be a lie. He hasn't heard or seen much of Wilt in a couple decades. But that doesn't matter. He knows Wilt is still there. Wilt can't die as long as the boy lives.

When will people understand that life and death are not as simple as we make them out to be? My encyclopedia says Mozart died in 1791. That's a damn lie. He is more alive now that he ever was. It says Van Gogh died in 1890. Horseshit. He's breathing like never before. Some people do die, no doubt about it. But there are others who do not, because they can't. No matter how deep the undertakers bury them, they come back to continue their walk across the planet earth.

Wilt Chamberlain scored a hundred points in one NBA game. He averaged fifty points a game for an entire season. He averaged more than twenty rebounds a game. No one has done this since. No one will do it in the future. Wilt is alive and well. Just ask the little boy from San Francisco. And what about Mozart?. The guy who wrote The Marriage of Figaro and the 21st Piano Concerto. I heard them both last week. And Van Gogh? I saw his sunflowers and watched his crows flying above the cornfields just yesterday.

Legends don't die. They float through transistor radios or shut eyes in warm beds and whisper good night to another day in paradise.

In the same pile of articles I found this piece Dad sent to the New York Times during the Clinton scandal. I think he sent it to the International Herald Tribune, too. I don't know if it ever got printed. Odds are it didn't. In the drawer there was only his typed copy.

BIG BILLY C. MISSES HIS BIG CHANCE

PRESIDENT BILLY C. IS A WONDERFUL MAN. He wouldn't be where he is if he wasn't extraordinary. He has everything going for him. He's tall, handsome, well educated, rich, and has a beautiful white house in

Washington. And when he talks, people listen. Like the 66,000,000 who were glued to their TVs last week when he told everybody about Monica.

When sixty-six million people are listening that is an occasion to say something worthwhile. Billy C. didn't. He blew it, very differently than how Monica blew it.

Billy C. should have told the facts. Not the facts about how he was getting his rocks off in the Oval Office. But the facts about men, the facts about how men who don't get their rocks off go crazy.

Billy C. probably hasn't rolled in the hay with his lawful wedded wife for 10 years. So what was he supposed to do? Go crazy? Masturbate in the shower every morning? Of course not. Nobody wants a crazy president. For Billy C. to be a good president he needs to get his rocks off. For any man to be a good man at whatever he does, he needs to get is rocks off. Every man knows this.

But very few admit it.

Billy C. should have admitted it.

Billy C. should have looked Puritan America in the eye and said, "Ladies and gentlemen, we Americans have got a serious institutional problem. The institution is marriage and the problem is what to do when a husband and wife stop exchanging juices.

Something has to change. Now I'm a man and I'm speaking for men. Women must have their own speakers. But I know that if I don't get my rocks off every week or so, my body starts beating up my brain. I don't function well. And as your president I need to function well. Monica was an angel. She helped me stay on top of my job. She kept me happy. She kept me feeling good about the country and myself. I wish to take this opportunity to thank Monica publicly for all she has done—for me and for the United States of America.

"Now I know we Americans have trouble facing this music. But I also know that what I say is true for men. So I have decided, as your president, to propose a new amendment to our great constitution. We have an amendment about the right to bear arms. We need one about the right to bear gonads. We will all be happier. Men will be happier. Women will be happier. Our children will be happier. So I have decided to propose the following addition to our sacred constitution:

All men shall have the right to a nice safe orgasm at least every ten days, more often if circumstances allow.

"Now I know some of you women out there in

America might think this isn't fair. But don't worry. My lovely wife Hilary is working on an amendment for women, which shall be proposed in a week or so.

"Thank you for listening. And thank you Monica for helping me fulfill my duties to the utmost. Goodnight America and may Aphrodite bless you."

But Billy C. didn't say this. He said he had sinned.

No, you're right, I doubt that one got published. Let's redeem this chapter with a couple more.

BAD THREADS

"One should either be a work of art, or wear a work of art."
Oscar Wilde

THE DEPTH OF MY IDIOCY IS such that I think I'm the only person who doesn't age. This is because my eyes look at other people and not at myself. This is because years ago I stopped looking at myself. This is because during adolescence and my early twenties I looked at myself so much that boredom set in. Since then, I just look at other people and they are all getting older. I haven't changed for myself in forty years.

Part of my looking out at other people has included looking at sports attire. I have decided that most sports attire is very ugly. I don't understand why Yves St. Laurent, Pierre Cardin, Calvin Klein, and their friends don't make sports clothes. Sports clothes are only made by people like Nike and Reebok and Adidas and these people know nothing about aesthetics. They only know about shoes.

I have decided to give awards to the ugliest sports attire. Here are the winners of 1995 Ugliest Sports Clothes:

First Prize: Bicycle Racers' Outfits: Why would anyone want to look like a fluorescent fish with writing on it? But they do. Even the fifty-five-year-old men who go out in groups on Sunday morning choose to look like overgrown incandescent sardines.

Second Prize: Men's Swimming Apparel: Five hundred years ago Michelangelo explained very clearly that a man looks better with nothing on rather than wearing a piece of stretch nylon that creates the illusion a tennis ball is growing below his belly button. Why swimwear designers don't follow Michelangelo's very clear fashion guidelines is a mystery to me.

Bronze Medal: Fencing Uniforms. Fencers look like astronauts trying to get honey out of beehives. I would suggest painting their clothes with different colors like we do with Easter eggs. Every participant should have a different look. Only the sword is necessary to let the public know they're doing fencing.

Fourth Prize: Ice Hockey Helmets. These things would make Brad Pitt look like a retard. Ice hockey is such a virile sport, yet these hats make all the players appear to be brainless infants dressed by cruel grandmothers.

Well, these are the winners. I know many of you are saying I should have put long basketball shorts on my list. But no, they save guys like me whose thighs look like they belong to ostriches. At least that's how mine looked the last time I examined them in a mirror a few decades ago. And I'm sure they haven't changed.

REDEMPTION IN STUPIDITY

STUPIDITY IS NOT ALWAYS A BAD THING. It can be a saving force. It can make whole civilizations feel good about themselves.

When George W. Bush climbs on top of the mountain and proclaims "Freedom" to be the grand virtue of the world, he is propounding stupidity. But his sheep suck on his words and feel good about themselves. George's "Freedom" is a freedom to do what George and his government allow people to do. But Mexicans are not "free" to cross the Texas border. Kurds are not "free" to swim into Italy. A victim of a terrorist bomb is not "free" to do anything anymore.

To proclaim people are free in this world is to babble stupidities. But America feels redeemed as its leaders talk about "democracy and the free world".

In order to feel good about ourselves we believe wonderful stupidities that have nothing to do with reality. Our ignorance redeems us. We look at the stars and think they shine for us.

The fans in Real Madrid watch Zidane and think he is playing for them. Los Angeles Laker fans watch Kobe Bryant and think he is playing for them. But a moment's reflection reveals that Zidane and Kobe are playing for money because Madrid and Los Angeles are where the gold mines are. When Real and the Lakers win their fans feel redeemed. But their redemption comes from their stupidity.

Will the day come when we learn to feel good about ourselves without notions like "Freedom", "Heaven" and "Victory"? Wouldn't it be nice to be redeemed without silly vacuous myths?

Or maybe man's principal virtue is his blindness?

I must have read five hundred of these articles last week, everything that was in that big bottom drawer. I don't know how many pieces he burned or threw away. There were very few from his early years with the paper. He wrote a couple times a week for over three decades, so he put out about three thousand articles. Then, a year ago, he said he had nothing more to say and he quit the newspaper.

8

What's left of my father is now decomposing in the Mont-sûr-Rolle cemetery and resting peacefully in the fifteen Chiquita banana boxes upstairs on the attic floor. I gave his clothes, furniture, and the kitchen things to the Salvation Army. There might be a few straggling pieces of him with some of his old friends or loyal readers, but nothing that I know about. Yesterday, when I shut the door to his apartment for the last time, it finally hit me that he was dead, dead with a capital "D". I had the last box in my arms and as I got to the door I turned and looked back at what had been his home for twenty years. The emptiness was filled with the afternoon light and the white walls looked whiter because of the emptiness. A cold chill navigated my spine. The Lamb had finally been slain.

When I got home I felt like a tired fish hooked at the end of a line that wanted someone to reel it in and lay it in a basket. But my girlfriend was gone with the dogs for their afternoon walk. In the kitchen there were two letters on the counter. One was from Barbara Chardon and the other had no name or return address, only a postmark from Paris. I opened Barbara's first. It was written on a card with a big red rose on the front.

Dear Adam,

Please forgive me for taking so long to thank you for the great funeral. I know that sounds funny – "a great funeral" – but it really was. I'm not quite sure how Peter and I got home, but we made it.

I was looking through my cupboards the other day and found something of your father's I thought you might want to have. It's a thick old navy blue sweater that he used to wear a lot. He let me borrow it one chilly night and I forgot to give back to him. You can come and get it anytime or I'll bring it to you. Just give me a call – 021 728 45 62.

Hope you are well. All the best,
Barbara Chardon

I won't lie. After seeing those pictures my father had of her, the effect of reading the letter was a little somersault in the groin. One thing was sure: I would fetch that sweater. The question was when. Should I wait a few days before calling Mademoiselle Chardon? What made me think it would make any difference to her when I came?

I poured myself half of a beer and opened the other envelope. Inside was a postcard of a Dufy reproduction and this message:

Nov. 26

Dear Adam, Just a quick note to tell you that I'll be in Lausanne for Christmas (not for a funeral this time!) and if you're in town, it would be a pleasure to see you again. I'll call you when I'm there.

Best wishes, Louise Mauron

It took me a few seconds to put two and two together, but I realized that Louise was Lou-Lou, the woman at the funeral who lived in Paris and took me back to my father's grave at the end of the evening in Mont-sûr-Rolle. She was a classy woman and I hoped I'd get to see her again.

When my girlfriend came in, I told her about standing at the door of my father's apartment with that last box in my arms and feeling his death to the bone. As I watched her reaction I wondered if death was something that couldn't be shared. I didn't say anything about the letters and she didn't ask. We were pretty good about keeping out of each other's business. I think she sensed that I was feeling lost and she did something she rarely does; she invited me to join her in bed for "a nap". I accepted in a heartbeat knowing it would be more than a snooze.

I woke up an hour and a half later feeling giddy. My girlfriend wasn't in the bed. It was dark outside. November was pulling the shutters down on the day as the clock struck five. I went to the window. The Lausanne-Geneva Express blew by giving the house a gentle shake. Not only did the trains not bother me, but I had come to like them. There was something heartwarming about seeing clusters of humanity safely whisking by at a hundred and twenty kilometers an hour, all alive and warm with heads cozily framed in a window, and all with somewhere to go.

I walked out of the bedroom and called to my girlfriend. She was upstairs sewing and shouted back, "I'll be down in a few minutes…maybe half an hour!" I went into the living room and sat in the leather armchair next to the fireplace. There were five books on the table next to me waiting to be read. I picked up

The Complete Works of Edgar Allan Poe, thumbed through it, and put it down. Ditto with a biography of George Orwell and an obscure novel by Balzac in French. Maybe it was post-coital depression, but I felt empty and lonely. I had noticed over the years how such a feeling often followed intense orgasms, but I'd never talked to anyone about it. I might be wrong, but I don't think women experience it like men do. I had inherited my father's good humor, so whenever I sensed a cloud of melancholy rolling through me, I always wondered what brought it on. Real causality is a tough tangerine to peel, but over the years it did seem that in my case lovemaking was usually followed by a brief hollowness and gloom that I knew never lasted too long.

My girlfriend and I have been together for five years now. I've been back in Switzerland for sixteen, since finishing my university degree in Arizona. You're probably wondering what I do — for a living, that is. Yes, I have job, but it's nothing that a hundred other people couldn't do if I left tomorrow. I'm a translator at the Haute Institut des Relations Internationales — the Institute of International Relations — in Geneva. They have documents, I translate them. From French to English. From English to French. I'm just the convenient village idiot that knows two languages and can flip-flop from one to the other. Sometimes I translate orally at conferences. That's hard work, but I rarely do it. They know I prefer the written stuff. What's good about that is that I make my own schedule. Sure, there are deadlines, but I can pretty much shoot them down as I want to. The pay is good and it gives me gobs of free time. But I sensed that now my father had died the free time would continue to feel more like a burden than a blessing. I often find myself wandering around and wondering what to do or where to go. Should I read Poe or Balzac? Should I even read? Should I walk out the door and go to Tahiti? Should I go into the kitchen and start fixing dinner? Should I forget about waiting to call Barbara Chardon and call her right now? Should I go upstairs and ask my girlfriend if she wants to get off the pill such that we can make a baby so I won't be so alone on the earth? Should I go for a walk or drive up to Mont-sûr-Rolle and say hello to Charley Lamb and his neighbors (I hadn't been back since the funeral)? Should I walk five steps to the stereo system and put on Dvořák's cello concerto? Should I go sit on the train tracks and wait for the next train to take me to never-neverland? Should I let the dogs keep barking at passersby out front in the garden or should I let them in…? When you think about it, too much time to think can be a burden. My guess is that most creatures don't really think all that much. They do what they do, but don't ask why. Their lives – and their brains – are a pattern and they follow it. Their minds tell them what to do and they do it. Who do you know who questions what his or her brain tells him or her what to think, believe, and do? For some reason, since we buried Dad, these kinds of questions keep popping up. Does the brain control me or do I control the brain? It's a lot like with those morning stiffies: where do they come from? why at four-thirty? why later these days? who's running the show? which body parts command and which follow…?

I opened the door to let in the dogs. Their barking might have been pissing off the neighbors, especially the cute couple next door to the south. They remind me of Laurel and Hardy. He's short and round and she's tall and thin. He used to be an undertaker, but now he works for the police. He never talks about his job. He seems to spend all his free time working in the garden and fixing up his house. Everything is immaculate. Even his garage looks like the cleaning woman just came by, except they don't have a cleaning woman. He scrubs his tools like people scrub pots and pans. I'm the opposite. My garden is a mess; my garage looks like the city dump. I don't fix things until they are broken. And then I rarely repair them. I just find a place in the garage where they can live quietly until somebody throws them away. Why are my neighbor and I so different? The mystery lingers everywhere.

The dogs came thundering in, spun around a few times, barked at the pleasure of seeing me again, flicked furniture with their tails, then looked at me as if they were hungry. The three of us paraded to the kitchen and I tossed them a handful of dog biscuits. I poured myself the other half of the beer and went back my favorite chair in the living room.

If nothing else, I do try to be honest with myself. I wouldn't be having these groin somersaults thinking about Barbara Chardon if my girlfriend and I were still deeply in love. We're not; we've become like comfortable furniture for each other. After five years we rarely make love. It's almost become medicinal. When one of us isn't feeling so hot, the other will try to be the drug that lifts the spirits. Like my girlfriend did an hour ago. We can still make a fire; but it won't burn for very long. I know myself: when I really love someone, I don't think about other women. And we men are slaves to our hormones. At least I am. I admit it. Remember, I pretend to try to know myself. Be honest with myself. Which should mean being honest to others. Am I honest with my girlfriend? How does one ever know? Hasn't it been proven over and over that when lovers move in together, their relationship changes? When my girlfriend and I lived apart, moments together almost always ended up in bed in a coital position. Now that we live together the bed is used for sleeping. It's nobody's fault. My dirty clothes don't inspire eroticism. Her desire to sit in front of the TV every night doesn't turn on my copulative engines. So what has happened? Where are we now? Things like visions of Barbara Chardon lounging in lingerie begin fertilizing my brain. Should I tell my girlfriend? Why? That would be being stupid more than being honest. We all have our private worlds and fantasies. But when one is deeply in love, does one fantasize? Can you imagine Romeo or Juliet fantasizing about somebody else? Hell no. Is there a solution? Should we stay together or split? We live comfortably together for sure. But the passion has seeped into the woodwork. Sometimes I think I should take a lesson from Gauguin and, before it's too late, get on the first boat – or plane – to Tahiti and live what's left of life like…like what? A palm tree? A French painter? A surfer? A gigolo? I'm sure I'd be unsatisfied there too after a while. Gauguin came back, didn't he?

Sometimes I think what's wrong with most of us – me at the top of the list – is that we see life as a problem to be solved. We think there is a solution to life. We think there really is a "right way" to live. Haven't we all been bombarded with such an idea since we were old enough to walk? Do this; it is good! Don't do that; it is bad! But maybe life follows no such logic…

It was fully dark outside. The dogs were quiet next to my feet on the carpet. I got up to put on the Dvořák concerto. I don't know why my father didn't include it in his going away party because it's a killer, too. I've got a Karajan version with Rostropovich on the cello. It strikes me as music that was written by somebody who was perfectly suspended between life and death and who, when the chips were down, chose life.

The music was in its lugubrious middle when my girlfriend came downstairs. She suggested we go up to the Restaurant de la Tour for a pizza.

9

The next morning I called Peter Pittet at the newspaper, not to see how things were clicking with Barbara Chardon, but to ask him if he knew anything about my maternal origin. For some reason, with Dad dead, the long-lost Mom had begun to take on a different status. I suddenly wanted to know if I really was a cosmogonal orphan or if perhaps a mother was out there somewhere? He said he was writing a piece on women's weightlifting, but needed a break and suggested we meet at the Café Lorado in an hour. Before hanging up he declared, "I think we should admit once and for all that there are more than two sexes."

Pittet was at an age when he surely could have

retired, but he was one of those newspaper writers who would probably keep his paws in the ink until his toes hit the grave. He always had something to say. I found him seated in a corner of the Lorado, a Pastis in one hand, a cigarette in the other.

"Adam Lamb," he said, "son of the great Charley Lamb. Good to see you're still alive."

"The feeling is mutual," was all I could think to say. Then, "Thanks again for coming to my father's funeral."

"Thank you. Not only was it the best music I've ever heard at a funeral, but the post-game show was about as good as it gets."

"Glad to hear it. I think it was what Dad wanted."

"I'm sure it was. It took two of us to drive home, but we made it in one piece."

"As far as I know, everybody else did too," I said not mentioning Barbara Chardon's name.

"What do you want to drink? I'm having a Pastis."

It was eleven o'clock in the morning. "I'll have a cup of coffee."

"So what is it you want to see me about, Adam? I never had a son. It's always a pleasure to talk to you. No matter how you look at it, sons and daughters are different."

"I'm not there yet in life, Mr. Pittet. No kids."

"Peter. Peter for Charley. Peter for you. I'm glad my parents named me 'Peter'. I always liked it better than 'Pierre'. I don't know why. My English is terrible, but I prefer the English name to the French." He interrupted himself to tell the waitress about my coffee. "So what's on your mind Adam?"

"A lot of things." I hesitated. "You know, Mr…Peter, I think you were one of the few people my father truly liked in this world. He often claimed he loved humanity in general, but had trouble loving it in particular. You were one of the exceptions."

"Not many people knew him like I did. He was a cross between a raging bull and a gentle lamb. His name fit him like an old pair of jeans."

"I guess he didn't have a lot of people he could really talk to."

"He once told me you can't tell everything to a male friend because if you tell him you're having problems with your wife or girlfriend, the next thing you know he'll have his nose between her thighs." He laughed like a kid at his own joke, and then added, "I knew quite a bit about his mind, but not too much about his women."

"Well – actually – that's what I wanted to talk to you about. Not his women in general, but the one who hatched me."

"That one I never knew."

"I think you do know that my father and I always lived alone together until I went away to the university in America. Then he got married. Twice."

"Yeah, he was writing for the newspaper then. With you gone he needed some company."

"You might not know this, but in all our years together he never really told me anything about who my mother was."

"He never told me anything about her either."

"The only thing he ever said to me – and I'll never forget it – was: 'She left our world when you were a baby.' That's exactly how he put it, she 'left our world'. Every time I asked him about her – which wasn't often – he would get quite emotional, so I stopped asking. I was just wondering if he had ever opened up to you? Since he died, I have suddenly begun to wonder if she's alive."

"Which is understandable." He sipped his Pastis and lit another cigarette. "Adam, now that I think about it, once we were bullshitting about old love affairs and he said something like, 'Peter, if you had ever met Adam's mother, you would have tried to have your pecker in the oven by sundown.' A typical Charley crack. But that's all he said. No details about anything. Just a joke."

As the waitress approached with my coffee, Pittet gulped down the rest of his Pastis and ordered another. He looked at me with a sort of fatherly tenderness, so I asked, "How many children do you have, Peter?"

"Two. Two girls. Both married and gone a long time ago. One lives in England and the other in the south of France, in Nice. When the second one left home, my wife left, too. She had had enough of me. I guess it was reciprocal. But it was a decent marriage."

Neither of us spoke for a few seconds, then I said, "I've been cleaning out his apartment these days and going through everything he had in the place. Maybe I shouldn't have looked at his private stuff, but I couldn't help it."

"Adam, as much as I love the son of a bitch, he's dead...and you're alive. If you want to find out who your mother is, that's your business, not his. All he probably cares about now is whether or not there's snatch in paradise.... Did you find anything?"

"No, not really. There were a few letters from women, but no reference to a baby or a child. I found some pictures I hadn't seen of myself as a little kid. At least I think the kid was me. I was maybe a year old, but I was always either alone or with him, except in one where I was in the arms of a woman. You see my face and the back of her head. That's all."

Pittet stared at his fresh glass of Pastis as if he were trying to divine something out of the cloudy liquid. "You'd think he'd at least have kept a picture or two of the woman who was your mother."

"There were lots of pictures of women. (I wondered if Pittet had poked his own camera at Barbara Chardon's waves, valleys, and peaks.) Yes, lots of them. But nothing else with what might have been me in it."

"The son of a bitch always wanted those women for himself!" He chuckled. "But he and I both knew that one way or another they almost always slither away into somebody else's garden."

I could see more and more why he and my father got along so well. They were both top-of-the-line bullshitters. And realists deluxe. He was as easy to talk to as Charley Lamb had been. I finished my coffee, licked my upper lip, and said, "Well, it's not the end of the world if I don't know who hatched me. I've gone forty years without knowing, so I guess I can go forty more."

"Hell, everybody wants to know who their mother and father are. One thing's for sure…there are a hell of a lot more unknown fathers than mothers. In today's world, half the known fathers today aren't probably the real ones." He laughed, then added,

"Mothers have always had an advantage when it came to knowing genealogical trees."

I watched Pittet sip his drink and scratch the back of his neck. I watched him think. His eyes and mouth turned more serious. "Adam, did you ever see that old Fellini film called Satyricon?" He didn't wait for me to answer. "There is a part in it I've never forgotten. It took place during the fall of the Roman Empire. There was this beautiful young teenage boy who was just wandering around all the time. He had no family. No roots. No sense of being a part of anything. Rome was chaos. All of a sudden, I realized how absolutely crucial it was for humans to have a sense of history and belonging. We all have to situate ourselves in the universe. Families do it. Friends do it. Religions do it. Political parties do it. Nations and cities do it. Sports and clubs do it. Genealogy does it. We all want to know who we are…. It sounds silly. It sounds simple. But it might be one of the most 'human' things in existence. For you, Adam Lamb, to want to know from whose womb you popped is as understandable as wanting to know if God exists. Unfortunately I have no idea about either subject."

Pittet gave me that fatherly look again. Then he checked his watch and said he needed to get back to the office and finish the piece on female weightlifters.

As he raised a finger to get the waitress's attention to pay, he said, "Did you ever check your birth certificate? That might tell you something."

"I tried once, many years ago. I asked my father about it. All he gave me was a paper from the U.S. State Department, "Certification of Birth Abroad", and on that there is no mention of parents' names. Just my name, where I was born, when, and a consul's signature."

As we walked to the door he said, "Let's get together soon."

"Sure," I responded, and I watched the man who might have been my father's best friend do a little jitterbug as he made his way through traffic to the tall copper building on the other side of the street.

10

Barbara Chardon lived near the lake in Pully, the town just east of Lausanne. When she told me her address, I knew exactly where it was. Long ago my father had often taken me to a little stretch of sandy beach in Pully where I would play and he would read. We would always park the car on a quaint street lined with elm trees, the Chemin de Villardin, and then would walk across the main road to "our beach", as my father called it. So when Barbara Chardon said, "Chemin de Villardin 18," my mind flicked on a quick slideshow of summer warmth and my father taking towels and toys in one hand, me and a book in the other and the two of us skipping across the Avenue Général Guisan to the calm and safety of the path next to the lake. We must have started going there when I was three or four years old. At least I have a vision of sometimes being "carried" toward the spot. Later I remember my father squeezing my wrist as we ran together across the road. "Our beach", I eventually came to realize, was a rarity around Lake Geneva for a couple of reasons. First, it had a little sand, and second, it was located at a place where the lake cut back in a gentle "U-shape" and hence was somewhat protected and warmer than other "beaches". There were two green benches set back against a high wall that separated the area from the mansions behind. My father used to sit there reading while I frolicked in the sand and the knee-deep water. He always seemed to have one eye on me and one eye on his book. Sometimes he would lay the book on the bench, rise and take off his shirt, and join my kingdom of castle building. I had a red pail and a yellow shovel and that was all we needed. There were always pieces of slick wood that had washed up on the shore to decorate and fortify our palaces. Sometimes I would build one and my father would build another and we would tell each other stories about what was going on in each other's castle. If we had a war, he'd figure out a way to lose. It's funny, but I don't remember other people ever being on our beach. They were there, of course, sunbathing or throwing sticks for their dogs. But they were not there for me. It was always "our beach".

Barbara Chardon lived on the third floor of a three-story building on the west side of the Chemin de Villardin. I saw this – the third-floor location – on the line of mailboxes just inside the entrance. I got there just before dark on a rainy December afternoon. There was no elevator and the stairwell was poorly lit making it was difficult to read the names on the doors. The building was quiet until I reached Barbara's door. Bob Dylan was singing behind it. I didn't think anybody listened to Bob Dylan anymore. It was the Lay Lady Lay ballad. (An omen?) I pushed the bell. Nothing. I rang it again a little longer. Dylan shut up. Barbara Chardon appeared.

She was wearing brown jeans, a baggy black sweater, and thick grey socks. Without her boots on she was still tall and still had the catwalk swagger as she led me past the kitchen to the living room. The room was reasonably spacious, but sparsely furnished: a long orange couch, a shaggy beige rug, a low glass table, and a couple of wooden crates set side by side for her music system. This was an apartment of someone who wasn't – or didn't want to be – encumbered by "stuff". It looked as though, if the inkling struck her, she could move out of the place in ten minutes. She pointed to the couch. I sat down on one end and she curled up on the other.

"Any trouble finding the apartment?"

"Not at all. I know the street. It's a nice neighborhood. My father used to bring me to the little sandy beach down on the lake."

"Really? I go there myself quite often. Especially in the spring. It's always warmer there than any other place because it's sort of protected and has the sun reflecting off the water all afternoon."

"My father used to call it 'our beach'."

"Small world I guess."

"How long have you lived here?"

"Five or six years. I moved in here after I got divorced."

"I didn't know you had been married."

"How were you supposed to know?"

It was a good question. "I don't know," I said dumbly.

She smiled. "Yeah, I got married on my twenty-seventh birthday. He was a rich Greek who had what people call everything…on the outside, that is — money, good looks, fast cars, a yacht in St. Tropez, pretended to know the wine lists like preachers the Bible. All that kind of thing. He told me we were going to Las Vegas for my birthday. We went, hit the shows, drank too much champagne, and the next thing I knew we were headed into one of those portable churches where he threw a tooth-sized diamond at me. Within twenty minutes, I became Mrs. Georges Papadopoulos. The problem with the marriage was that I eventually got to know the inside of the guy. And the problem with that was that there was no inside."

"There had to be some sort of core in there," I said thinking I should at least try to give the guy a chance. (At what? Not being an asshole?)

"Well, Adam, there was nothing I could find." (The fact that she called me "Adam" made me feel good.) With that, like a slinky ocelot, she uncurled and stood up. "I forgot to ask what you'd like to drink."

"Anything is fine."

"How about a little Porto. Your father loved Porto in the winter. He used to say Porto was to Christmas what white wine was to Easter. He was kind of right."

As she loped toward the kitchen, I wondered if my father went so uncomplainingly toward death because after Barbara Chardon there wasn't much left to do. But it could have worked the other way around, i.e. after tasting this giant cookie, a man would do everything possible to stay alive to taste it again.

She came back with two glasses of Porto and a bowlful of mixed nuts. As she resumed her knees-to-chest position on the couch, I rekindled the conversation, "So you didn't stay married for long?"

"It took two years before I was finally free of the guy. I lived with him for a year. We split. For six months he kept sending me rose bushes and diamond mines and perfume factories trying to get me back. Then it took another six months to get the divorce finalized. It was quite quick actually because I didn't want any of his money. I did learn something from the marriage, so I can't say I really regret the whole thing. And as Charley used to say, 'What doesn't kill you should make you stronger.' With Georges Papadopoulos it was boredom that was killing me. We had absolutely nothing to talk about. My father had told me – when I was about twenty years old – that if I decided to get married one day I should remember that I'd have to look at the man's face every morning across the breakfast table. What he forgot to tell me was that I'd have to talk to the guy! Anyway, I learned that there is nothing worse in a relationship than boredom. When I met Charley at my uncle's funeral it was like suddenly the alphabet had more than two letters, if you see what I mean."

"Sure."

So here it is. Let's be straight. As straight as possible. Let's pretend you are me. It's a cool dark wet December late afternoon and you're sitting on an orange couch with the closest thing you've ever met to a siren. A mermaid. A nymph. Not only is she gorgeous, she's amusing, witty, charming, and she knows how to smile and laugh and not worry about her fucking beauty all the time. Not only is she amusing, witty, charming, and knows how to laugh, but you know the body breathing calmly beneath her clothes is also a chiseled gem. You've seen it in black and white and in Technicolor in your father's collection of pictures. You're a male. You're a goddamned man with all the machinery and juices inside you that nature has so generously provided. This woman has already made your loins flip-flop, and now you're sitting in her living room and she is a mere four feet away from you. You can even smell her subtle peppery lemon-tinted perfume. And then there's the aspect of your father. This woman was your father's girlfriend. She passed through his fingers and he through hers. And not all that long ago. Does this matter? Do you recoil from a comparative assessment? Or do you profit from your genetic association? You wonder why he never told you about her, or why he rarely said a word about any of his female companions, and if you ever do get to the bottom of this human angel, will you somehow be desecrating your father's confidence? Or, on the other hand, will he be applauding from his grave and cheering you on to a thrilling victory? Go Adam, Go! Two Bits, Four Bits, Six Bits a Dollar, All for Adam's Cane Stand Up and Holler! And he'll bump his head on his stupid coffin…! And then there is the element of your own girlfriend. What do you do there? Are you loyal or not? Aren't all good relationships based on loyalty? Maybe yours isn't so good. If it were perfect you know you wouldn't seek other women. But how many relationships are perfect? If you touched Barbara Chardon, would that make you a schmuck? Maybe you're already a schmuck for just thinking about the possibility? And what about your girlfriend? Are you sure she doesn't seek other men? Should that matter? Would her disloyalty be the only thing that could justify yours? Shouldn't your moral principles not depend on what others do? If the two of you have had a fight, or are a little bored with each other, should that change anything? Or if you haven't made love for a few weeks or months? And if you don't seek other women, do you hand over your life to frustration, castration, and decrepitude? Has any man on the face of the spinning earth ever not sought other women? What do you do? Are your mind and body always on the same page? Should they be? Who are you? What are you? … As you sip the Porto, you warm up. The siren doesn't have a fireplace, but she doesn't need one. She is the fireplace. You feel the heat coming horizontally. You feel it coming vertically from below. You feel the slug's head poke skyward. There is only a meter and some change of space between you and this long-finned mermaid. She is now running her tongue along her lower lip bringing an errant drop of her drink into her mouth. And her mouth looks rested, but hungry. Like maybe she was waiting for YOU. So what do YOU do – 'you' all-knowing all-seeing reader? What would 'your' next move be? There you are. It's all laid out like a Thanksgiving table. What in heaven and earth's name do you do? Does the fact that you most probably only live once come into play? … And do you know what? I'll tell you what. The worst of it is that you – or I – don't really know what we will do until we have done it. That's the funny part of it all.

So here's what I did. I set my glass of Porto on the table. Then I lowered my hand into the bowl of mixed nuts and put a few in my mouth and chewed them. Then I picked up my glass of Porto again and sipped.

Then I licked some salt off my upper lip. Then I looked at Barbara Chardon and said, "What are you doing now?... I mean for a living that is?" And she said, "I sell things over the phone. It's the most ridiculous job in the world. But it's better than living with Georges Papadopoulos." And I said, "Can you choose your own hours?" And she said, "That's why I do it." And I said, "Me, too, I'm a translator, and that's why. Because I get up whenever I want and go to bed knowing that I can." Then she said, "You know, if I didn't know you were Charley's son I doubt I'd have guessed it. I mean by what you look like and all. The nose, eyes, ears, mouth...just about everything is different. Plus you're taller than he was." "I guess I take after my mother." "You must. Charley once told me she was a beautiful woman." "He did? Did he say anything else?" "No, he just said she'd been gone a long time, and I didn't push him for more information." "I never knew her. I mean I don't remember her." "Oh. I didn't know that."

Barbara Chardon went to the kitchen and fetched the bottle of Porto. She bent over and half refilled our glasses. When she repositioned herself on the couch she was no longer curled up and she was closer to me.

Outside we could hear the pitter-patter of rain falling on the darkness.

11

CREATIONISM, EVOLUTIONISM, DOG WALKINGISM
—Charles Lamb

THERE IS A WORLD. OUR WORLD. Some of us wonder how it got here.

If I understand the debate correctly, the good people in Kansas (and elsewhere) follow the Biblical lead and are convinced that God created the whole show a few thousand years ago. Who created God doesn't seem to arise as a question. It must be assumed that either He (She) (It) was always there or else He created Himself.

The evolutionists maintain that over a much longer period of time things evolved and evolved and evolved to where they are now. It seems another Charles, a Mr. Charles Darwin, helped father this idea and maintained a "survival of the fittest" position. The theory also implied that creatures "adapted" to their environments in such a way that they furthered their chances of "surviving" a little longer than they otherwise would have. A concomitant theory purports that this all started with a large bang. What happened before the explosion seems to be ignored.

I have a dog that I walk every day in a forest that has a river running through it. The setting is conducive to thinking about questions like, "Where did it all come from?"

I've been dog walking for ten years now and have wondered the following:

A. Don't most multiple-choice questions have more than two possibilities or at least a "None of the above"? Why is everybody so set on the creation-evolution dichotomy? Are Darwin and the Bible the only two possible solutions?

B. When it rains in my forest the slugs come out. They are essentially the same color as the ground and often get crushed by walkers.

Hence, the fact that they can hide in their environment (they blend in with ground) is also responsible for their deaths. Their being there, I think, might have nothing to do with a "survival of the fittest", but rather with a "survival of the luckiest". And when it rains their luck often runs out. Maybe they didn't evolve at all. If they did, shouldn't they be bright pink or yellow so we can see them on the path? But of course if they were a bright color other predators could see them more easily…Hmmm.

C. Don't both sides just beg the question? What was before God? If God has existed forever, couldn't everything else have existed forever, too? And – again – what was going on before the Big Bang banged?

D. Whoever said man had the capacity to know the answers to these kinds of questions in the first place? He doesn't even know where his wife was last night. How is he supposed to know what was going on a zillion billion trillion years ago? Why does man even care to know these things? My dog doesn't care and she's happy.

E. The search for truth is an admirable enterprise.

Or is it? It seems that it causes lots of unnecessary fights. And then there is Oscar Wilde's wisdom: "A truth ceases to be true when more than one person believes in it."

Oh well, the forest is beautiful and the dog loves to go therein. Every now and then I try to talk to her about my thoughts, but she just barks, sniffs, runs from tree to tree, or goes for a swim in the river.

AVEC LE TEMPS
—Charles Lamb

AS LIFE GOES BY, IT IS interesting to notice how certain interests die. I used to care about ski races. When Bernard Russi or Pirmin Zurbriggen were flying down the mountain I would anticipate Saturday morning, turn on the TV, and want them to win. Today, I never watch ski races. My life has come to a point where they mean nothing to me. There is a hole where a value used to be.

I used to follow American football. I knew the teams and the best players. Whenever I could, I listened to games on the radio, watched them on TV, or read about them in the International Herald

Tribune. Now the whole scene means as much to me as what brand of deodorant Napoleon used. Who wins and who loses is of no more importance than the name of the pig that provided the pork chop on my plate last night.

The same is true for tennis. A herniated disc came. I stopped playing, stopped watching, and slowly tennis disappeared from my Weltanschauung.

As life goes on, what once mattered doesn't anymore. Not only in sports, but also with books, music, even friends. I have a cupboard full of 33 tour records I don't listen to anymore. People like Rod Stewart, Mick Jagger, and Bruce Springsteen. I have shelves of books I haven't looked at for decades. I have dozens of addresses and phone numbers of people I never contact and probably never will again.

The world turns, and we turn with it. Getting older is, in a sense, weeding out a very vast and complicated world and holding on to a few sacred things. For me, ski racing, tennis, American football, and Rod Stewart are not among them.

As I look down the road a few years from now, I wonder what will be left...

GOD LIVES
—Charles Lamb

THE RECENT WORLD CUP FOOTBALL TOURNAMENT was important for me because it renewed my faith in God. Before Mr. Blatter's mammoth event I had feared God had disappeared. Watching the World Trade Center fall to the ground had made me wonder where God was. Then, watching the bombs fall on Afghanistan, I was forced to think that if God existed, He was on vacation. And I had also seen a lot of pictures of starving people in Africa which made me think if God can't even make rain, what can He make?

Then came the World Cup. When the Italians won, they thanked God for their victory. The players from Senegal did the same. Many players and fans assured me that God was responsible for their victories. *At least He cares about something,* I thought. When the Italians lost, if I remember correctly, it was because of the referees, not God. I wondered why God hadn't influenced the referees to save the Italians from their humiliation. Maybe that day was a holiday, thought I. If I remember correctly, when Senegal lost, the Senegalese said it was what God wanted. I had thought He was always on the winning side, but maybe not.

Then came Brazil. Brazil won and everyone was thanking God again. Except the Germans. They were wondering how Oliver Kahn could drop the ball in front of Ronaldo's foot. But the Brazilians said God was in Ronaldo's foot.

Anyway, the World Cup 2002 was a highly religious experience for me. It gave me new faith that God has a mighty hand on the affairs of man.

WHAT I THINK
—Charles Lamb

OVER THE PAST MONTH HUNDREDS OF people have asked me what I think about what they call "the war" in Iraq. Since nobody listens, I'm going to repeat – in print – what I think.

First, I think this war is one of millions of wars that are going on every second that the earth continues to turn. The cows and pigs that are waiting to be slaughtered in slaughterhouses around the world are at war. And they are all losers. The chickens that are waiting to have their heads cut off so you and I can eat them are at war. The flies at your picnic table that you are going to swat are at war.

But these wars, like the one in Iraq, are not real

wars. A real war, like a real basketball game, takes two more or less equal sides that fight it out until there is a victor. It takes two to make a real war. In Iraq, there was only one.

There are also wars in families, in couples, in individuals. There are casualties everywhere.

Second, what surprises me most is the people I hear on all sides who think they know what is good for the world. They proclaim to know what is right and wrong, good and bad, just and unjust. People don't know what is good for their own families. They don't know what is good for themselves. How can anybody expect to know what is good for the world?

This reminds me of all the people who hang around the sports world and think they know what a coach should do and what is right for a team. These people don't have one percent of the information and knowledge that a coach has; but they think they know what he should do.

It is fascinating. That humanity can be this ignorant.

To Bush or not to Bush? This is the question. But is it really the question? Maybe the bigger question is "How ignorant are we?" Maybe the more we think we know, the stupider we are.

Third, I hate war. From the day I was eight years

old and saw a dachshund run over by a car – the head was here, the tail was there, in the middle there was a pond of blood – I have hated war. I almost went crazy then. Sixty-two years later I still might have time.

Before I left her apartment, Barbara Chardon gave me an envelope containing these four articles and a short story by my father that I had never seen before. The newspaper pieces I had read while cleaning out Dad's apartment. The story I had never seen.

The next morning I took it with me on a winter stroll down to the park by the lake. It was a sunny afternoon, so I sat on a bench next to the water and took it out of my pocket. Before I started reading, I closed my eyes for a few minutes and felt the sun and its reflection from the lake on my face. When I opened my eyes, I saw a blind man with a guide dog coming my way, his white cane tapping the smooth lakeside path in front of him. When they got a couple of meters from me the dog moved my way and pulled the man toward the bench. His stick discovered it before he bumped into it. Of course he didn't know I was three feet away.

"Oh Charlie," he said.

"I think the dog had just wanted to say hello," I offered. He smiled, said nothing, and they continued on their way.

I will never forget that moment – not because the dog had the same name as my father, but because of the comparative situation. There I was with eyes that showed me the majestic lake and beautiful Mont Blanc in front of me; there he was seeing nothing with a cane, a leash and a dog in front of him. That he had learned to navigate the park, the lake, and the river that runs into it was astounding. But he had. I was surprised he didn't say anything back to me. But he didn't. I thought about following him just to see how far he had to go to get home…to see where home was. The town of Morges held about fifteen thousand souls. I had never seen this man before. I would never forget him. The nearest apartment building was at least two hundred meters away. I imagined the reality of those meters for him and for me were two very different things.

For whatever reason, I stayed on the bench and read my father's story. The other "Charlie" was guiding the blind man home. All I could think about was how everybody experiences reality differently. And had I not just seen the blind man, I'm sure I would have read a different story, a tale that would have just reminded me of Bill Clinton and Monica Lewinsky.

THE NEXT WAR PLEASE

by Charles Lamb

This is what Arnold Baxter Crown thought as he was struggling, last night, in the year 2002, toward sleep in the bed he shared with his wife of twenty-two years: After the war on terrorism, I have a suggestion for whomever is president…. Start a war on the frustration of the loins. Millions of lives are lessened and unfulfilled because the volcano cannot go off in pleasant circumstances.

His proposed war would be on the behalf of men. Why? Because he was one. He knew what it felt like. "May a woman step forward after I shut up," thought he, "and declare her own war. We all have our battles to fight."

The war on the frustration of the loins would be a different kind of war. It would be a war unlike any we have had before. It would be fought in every abode from Seattle to Singapore to the South Seas. It would be the first real "world war".

Up until then the problem of frustration of the loins had been dealt with in weak guerilla fashion: men reading girlie magazines in bathrooms, soapy hands in showers, vacations to Amsterdam or

Thailand, clandestine mistresses, grungy titty bars next to highways, business trips that detoured to porno theaters and massage parlors. These were hit and miss guerilla tactics. They were Band-Aids on heart attacks. They were a few loaves of bread for the starving millions in Sudan. The problem had not been helped. Men continued to suffer. Why?

(Arnold rolled away from his wife who was reading a women's magazine in a dim light. He respected her right to read in bed and his right to sleep.)

Why did men suffer? First, he thought the origin of the problem had been completely misunderstood. The urges in male loins were not of a moral origin. They were not good or bad. They did not spring from evil or the Devil. They were simply there, built into the great cosmic fabric of the universe. Every male he knew felt them. Their rocks wanted to go off in spite of anything they might have thought, believed, or subscribed to. Barbers, governors, priests, presidents, postmen — all wanted to cut loose. And they wanted to cut loose frequently. Science had never determined exactly how frequently, but Arnold's guess was that there was something close to a 24-hour cycle (the same as an earthly rotation), which might diminish somewhat after seven or eight decades of living. The rumblings in the loins, like blood type or the color of eyes or the size of feet, were not a man's choice. They were simply there, in every man, like lungs or a liver or a spinal cord. And they were neither more nor less moral than a lung, a liver, or a spinal cord. They were as amoral and innocent as butterflies in spring…

Arnold's musings then led to his friend, Alfonse Berrywell Comely, whom he had met the week before. They had bumped into each other in a Do-It-Yourself shop and Alfonse had invited Arnold over for a drink. Arnold had said yes because he had had nothing better to do. Alfonse was twenty-five years older than Arnold; seventy-eight to be exact. They had often played tennis together before both their backs had started acting up. Alfonse lived in a big house inherited from his father a few miles north of Geneva. He had been a favorite of Coco Chanel who had hired him a half a century before to peddle her perfumes in Switzerland. He lived downstairs in the mansion in what had been a basement. His wife lived upstairs. They had separate entrances and separate keys. He really only talked to her when her kidneys started acting up. He never called her, only she wanted to maintain the dead couple's communication.

Alfonse sat Arnold down at a messy wooden table set between his kitchen and sitting room. He showed him a packet of photographs of young African women.

"I feel great," he said. "Never felt so good in my life. These are my women. Wouldn't touch a white woman again for as long as I live." Most of the women looked about twenty. "This is my favorite," Alfonse said pointing to a girl with jeans and a t-shirt. "She calls me 'The Tongue'. Says she's never met one like mine before."

Naturally Arnold was jealous. He, a quarter of a century younger, suffered in bed nightly next to a wife he rarely touched anymore. And here was Alfonse, almost dead, lighting up twenty-year-olds like fireworks on New Year's Eve.

Arnold drove home and started repairing the kitchen faucet. "Where have you been?" his wife asked.

"I met an old tennis buddy," he answered. "We had a drink together."

"Oh," his wife said.

That night Arnold didn't sleep well, but he hadn't as yet thought through his plan for the next war. He had simply ruminated about his dormant soft prick and wondered if any of Alfonse's African girls might have sisters. Sisters in the area, that is.

The following night Arnold remembered his "garagist", Albert Bugnon Clavel. He hadn't seen him for six months, but the last time he was there changing the oil, Albert had told him that he had just come back from Cameroon. "Why Cameroon?" Arnold had asked.

"Because twenty francs there is worth a thousand here."

"What do you mean?"

"I mean if you buy them an ice cream cone, they're satisfied."

"Who?"

"The women. They're satisfied and so are you. Here you have to buy them a fucking house and they're still looking for excuses. In Cameroon, they laugh, they smile, and they take peter pecker like it's a vitamin."

That was six months ago. Now, as he lay in bed like a cold brick, Arnold was thinking about his war on male frustration. He had erupted once in the last year and that was in a dream. And it had been more a drip than a lava flow. Should he write the President? Should he call him? Should he go through his congressman? But he didn't have a congressman. He hadn't lived in America for forty years. He didn't know the ropes anymore. He didn't even know the string. Arnold lay in bed, a freshly plucked fish in a basket, turning from side to side, going nowhere, waiting for a dumb death.

The next day at work – he was a printer – he shouted his idea to the guy at the machine next to his. "Hey, Andrew! I think we need a war! We need to free all the slaves! We're the slaves! When was the last time you scored?" Andrew Burris Constantini was in his late forties. He had a wife and two kids.

"If I told you, you'd laugh!"

"No I wouldn't!"

"Last Christmas! Santa Claus came!"

"Was it any good?"

"About as good as a raincoat in the Sahara Desert! And you?"

"Easter! The Easter Bunny hopped in bed with me! I tell you, we need a war!"

"Won't happen!" Andrew shouted. "Not enough women in the world!"

"Yeah there are! In Africa!"

When Arnold went home that night his wife was ironing in the living room and watching TV. "You don't need to iron my clothes anymore," he said.

"What do you mean? Of course I do."

"No, you don't. It doesn't matter."

"Of course it does. What's wrong with you? What's got into you?"

"Nothing. You just don't need to iron my shirts."

"Arnold, is something wrong? Are you all right?"

Arnold went to the bedroom and lay down. He looked at the ceiling. No, there will never be a war, he thought. And he was right. At least not in his lifetime, anyway.

12

We were all swimming into the vast ocean called "The Twenty-First Century". My father just got his toes wet. Three years and ten months' worth. He couldn't have cared less. Not about dying, but about the new century. Before hitchhiking to Europe in the late 1950s he had studied cultural anthropology at the University of California in Berkeley. He told me that in five years of studying the human race, he essentially learned one thing: Man is a sheep without the fur coat.

We talked about this when he took me to Venice in the spring of my sixteenth year. I remember because it was one of the few times Charles Lamb got a little serious in my presence. Normally he joked at this and played at that, be it cooking, cleaning, writing, car washing, tennis, basketball or ping-pong. He joked. We played. That trip to Venice seemed like the day before yesterday…

We had taken the morning train from Lausanne. Charley said he wanted my first look at Venice to be when the sun was going down. We'd get in at five-thirty that afternoon. It was the end of May and we had a compartment of six seats to ourselves. He had fixed a picnic for us. When we pulled out of Milano we started to eat. I had a soda and he uncorked a small bottle of Chianti. Halfway through his sandwich and the wine, for some reason, he started talking about his college education at Berkeley…

"Adam, you're sixteen years old and still haven't shaved and probably don't give a shit about any of this," was how he started the discussion. "But, I'll tell you anyway. We've got a few more hours in front of us, and when we get to Venice I want those eyes and that head of yours to be wide open…. I spent five years at the university – worked my ass off paying for it. I didn't want my parents to foot the bill. They had three other kids before me and one more after. They were part of the 'Let-God-Be-the-Contraceptive' generation, so from the age of seventeen on, I decided to stay out of their wallets. I think it's about time I tell you what I got out of my education."

"I'm all ears," I said. And I was. I couldn't help but tune in when he got serious.

"I decided to major in anthropology, the study of man. Big subject, right? Well, back then they limited it to either bones – 'Physical Anthropology' – or culture – 'Social Anthropology'. I chose the cultural stuff. And I'm glad I did. I've always thought the bones business was a farce. When I was a kid people were saying that the human race had been around for a few thousand years. Then, when I got to college, scientists found a few more skeletons and they started saying people had been walking the earth for around 20,000 years. The next thing you know they've upped the ante to 50,000. Today they're talking about a few million years. The moral of the story is that as far as I'm concerned, nobody has any idea how long human beings have existed. All the really old bones have turned to oil or pixie dust. My guess is that we've been around a whole lot longer than anybody will ever know. The fact is that people want to know where they came from. Hence they'll believe just about anything." He paused and looked at the Italian countryside flying by. He cut off a slice of apple and sipped his wine. Out the window I remember we started seeing more and more palm trees and orange, pink and faded yellow houses. It was my first time in Italy. Maybe it was the rumbling hum of the train, but I was in lighthearted mood.

"Nobody ever talks about anthropology in my school," I said.

"I'm sure they don't, but they should. Kids your age need to start understanding that people are herd animals that bah just like sheep…We're followers, Adam. We're all sheep. Have you ever looked at the kids in school? They dress the same, talk the same talk, carry the same bags, ride the same bicycles, play the same games, listen to the same music, believe in the same gods, disbelieve in the same gods, watch the same TV shows, follow the same rules, think the same things are cool, etcetera, etcetera. Of course there are variations within the culture. Some kids like The Beatles and some like Deep Purple, but you see what I mean. Very few, if any, jump out of their cultural quicksand. People follow tradition and fads. It's not a bad thing. I think it's a necessary thing. It's the way people are. Anthropology should be taught at a young age to get kids to start examining their values and traditions before it's too late. Kids need to understand that what they think is 'cool' is not necessarily cool for people in other cultures. What's cool in the middle of Africa ain't cool in New York. And what's cool in New

York ain't cool in Siberia. You get my point..."

"It's not too hard to understand."

"Bright kid."

"Thanks Dad." I remember I was munching on a big chocolate chip cookie he had bought in a bakery before we got on the train.

"Now," he went on, "there are a few other reasons to teach young people this stuff. First, it would help them stop thinking that their brand of jeans is the coolest brand on the planet. They might realize that in a few years their brand will give way to another brand and then in a few more years jeans will be out of style all together and people will be wearing knickers or Scottish kilts again."

"Come on, Dad..."

"Well, something different, anyway. I'll never forget when I was a kid – maybe eight or nine – and my mother bought me a raincoat that had cowboy fringe on the front. I couldn't wear that to school for a million dollars. Nobody in my town wore a raincoat with cowboy fringe on the front. Nobody. And I wasn't going to be the first. My dear mother got the scissors and cut the fringe off. I was able to slip into the school bus without taking any shit from Buzzie Grundel and Brian Tibbits. You get my point? We're sheep. We follow the cultural shepherds."

"Yeah…"

"I often wonder if Americans might be worse about this because their culture is so big and powerful that it's very hard for them to imagine that they're not the center of the damn universe. Which brings me to my second point…. Once people realize that their crap isn't the only crap, then they start to have a little more respect for other people's crap. If you realize your goddamned god isn't the only goddamned god, then you see that maybe, just maybe, what you believe in might not be the only thing to believe in, and, in fact, might not be the true thing to believe in. And once you respect the fact that other people's crap is just as sacred as your crap, then you're open to lots of other crap. You can observe other cultures, expand your horizons, drink other wines, listen to other music, hear a new idea or two, learn a new language, and all the rest."

He looked out the window. I remember thinking that I probably loved my father more than most sixteen-year-olds did. I never really rebelled against him because there was nothing to rebel about. He never tried to force anything down my throat…except not to be a close-minded asshole.

"That's really why I left America," he continued, "after I finished the university. I just wanted to add a few new chapters to the book of my life. I wanted to see new places, eat different foods, hear different voices, and maybe think about life in different ways. It wasn't easy in the beginning. Those first few months were lonely as hell."

"What did you do when you first got here?"

"I only had a few hundred dollars to my name. After wandering around Geneva for a couple of weeks, I found a job washing dishes in a restaurant. A few months later, I got lucky and found a job teaching English. I wanted to stay in Europe long enough to learn a new language and feel the blood and guts of another culture. I guess I did that. I've been here long enough to have had you, teach and write a newspaper column for twenty years."

I recall thinking it might have been a good moment to ask him about my mother. But he gulped down the last of the Chianti and said it was time for a nap. He pulled down the window shades in the compartment and drew the curtains. Then he tugged out the seats and made a makeshift bed. He rolled his jacket into a pillow and lay down like the gentle giant he was. Within minutes he was purring a snore – or snoring a purr. He didn't wake up until we pulled into Venice.

I will never forget what I saw when we walked out of

the train station: a plaza, no cars, a silent flow of people, a canal, a bridge, faded pinkish pastel buildings and palaces under a powdery blue sky. At the time I thought it was probably the most beautiful sight I'd ever seen in my life. It was as if Charley Lamb had planned it all to get his son to appreciate the world.

We stood there staring for a few minutes, then hopped in a vaporetto from the station down the Grand Canal. Every sixteen-year-old kid in the universe should do this, especially on a late afternoon in May in 198_, when you can sit next to your father in the front of the boat and there is nothing between your eyes and absolute beauty. The only sounds you hear are the up-and-down rumble of the engine, the boat gently bumping the dock at each stop, the whine of the thick worn ropes as they are wound in place to keep the vessel still for a couple of minutes while passengers get on and off, the choppy slap of water on walls, and the mewing of seagulls.

We got off next to a line of bouncing gondolas. My father hadn't told me anything about what to expect or what we were going to see. Of course I'd seen pictures of Venice and a few shots of the city in films, but my preconceived notions were minimal. As we walked past a magnificent palace and into the center of the Piazza San Marco, my eyes felt like they were on fire. This wasn't Disneyland; for centuries real people had lived and died here. It wasn't built for tourists; it was constructed for daily living of highly civilized people. My father saw lots of folly in mankind, but he had an enormous respect for what human beings had produced on this earth. There, in Venice, he had nothing but praise to pour on those who had envisioned and created such a city. "Can you imagine," he said more than once, "actual people built this place…a few hundred years ago! It is mind blowing." On the train, he had talked about the sheep. Here he was showing me the lions and the eagles.

We stayed in Venice for two nights. That was long enough. The light that got switched on in a corner of my brain has never gone off.

13

Christmas is coming. So is the regularity of my morning erections. I believe they are a good sign, a sign that I am healthy and at full strength, that I am running on all cylinders, that I want to live, that I have a dinosaur's urge to reproduce and perpetuate life. It doesn't necessarily mean that when the morning thrust isn't there I am in a bad state or that I am not feeling good about myself and the world. But when I wake up at four-thirty with a Chili Dog grinding the sheets, it is a sign that I am fully alive, ready to devour the day, ready to inhale the sugary scent of a woman, and to embed the organ into the sweet sylph lying next to me…. But it rarely happens anymore. My manhood is almost always left to cool, shrink, curl up, and return to its nest as its carrier falls back to sleep.

That's what happened this morning. (It's been a week since I went to Barbara Chardon's apartment.) When I got up I decided to call my father's old buddy, Danny Dapper. I knew he still lived in Geneva and I had to go to L'Institut de Hautes Etudes Internationales to take back a couple of translations and pick up some new ones. Usually the period around Christmas is slow, but because of the mess in Iraq they've been keeping me busy. Danny Dapper had taught at the Institute until he retired a decade ago. He was the one who set me up with the job after I finished my university studies in Arizona. He lives across the Pont de Mont Blanc in the Eaux-Vives neighborhood. I wanted to see if he might have a clue or two about the woman who gave birth to me. I rang him up and he told me to come by his place at noon and we could have lunch together.

Danny Dapper was probably born two or three years before my father, but he was hanging in there solidly. He showed few signs of decay. He kept a trimmed moustache and his streaky grey locks were wavy and neatly parted giving him an elderly Clark Gable-ish look. He was around five-feet-eight, not at all overweight, and always dressed like someone who cared about his appearance.

"Thanks for inviting me," I said sincerely after he opened the door. Then, I couldn't resist asking, "Mr. Dapper, is your name really Danny Dapper?" I asked as he ushered me inside. "That's all my father ever called you."

"Of course it isn't. Charley Lamb stuck the label on me. I was 'Danny Dapper' to him, but to the rest of the world I'm still Daniel Davenport, an old retired professor of moral philosophy. Some people even call me 'Doctor Daniel Davenport', but I can't cure anybody of any disease." He chuckled. "Your father gave me the 'Dapper' name because he was always jealous of my wardrobe. He didn't care what he wore – he and his moth-eaten sweaters and paint-stained jeans."

"Yeah, he was never much for new clothes."

While we were still standing in the hall, he suggested we go to his favorite pizzeria just down the street. "Anything is fine," I said.

As we walked to the restaurant I said, "Well, I always liked the name 'Danny Dapper'. When my father said it, it had a happy ring to it which made me think he liked you."

"To be liked by Charley Lamb was a great accomplishment. I miss him. I could talk to him."

"I know he liked talking to you, too."

"He enjoyed that Pittet fellow as well. I could see why at the post-funeral party. He's a real character."

"He always said close friends were hard to come by in this big wide world."

The pizzeria was already full of people, but Danny had reserved his favorite table. The menus were in our faces within seconds of sitting down.

"What would you like to drink, Adam?"

"A glass of white wine would be fine."

"Charley Lamb Junior. That's my boy. Your father drank enough white wine to fill Lake Geneva. By the way, I really did enjoy his funeral."

"Thanks. Everyone seemed to have had a good time. It was an interesting set of people."

"Absolutely. I had wondered who would come to the funeral, besides Pittet and myself that is. I should have known there would be a few interesting women. I enjoyed all of them. Your father never really talked much about his love life with me, but it seems he kept it alive until he was dead."

"Actually, Mr. Daven…"

"Call me Danny."

"Okay…Danny…Actually that's kind of what I wanted to talk about." The white wine came and we clinked glasses. "Not so much the women at the funeral, but about the woman who gave birth to me." He gave me a fatherly glance. I crawled on. "Since he died – since I'm in this orphaned state – I've started to wonder more and more about my mother. I'm not sure if you know this, but I never knew my mother and my father rarely mentioned the subject and I rarely brought it up. When you grow up without a mother, I guess you don't really miss her…"

"Yes, of course."

"Well, since my father died I've started to wonder more about who my mother was."

"Which is only normal, Adam."

We both glanced quickly at the menu and both settled on the plat du jour, *Lasagne fait maison.*

"Dad was dead…but I couldn't help thinking that maybe Mom might still be alive somewhere…anywhere."

"Adam, in all honesty, I don't know anything other than the fact that you were born a few years before I got to know your father. I think you were eight or nine when I met him. You were the only thing he loved more than women. And believe me, he loved women. He said many times he was a slave to female beauty. But he loved you even more. You could smell his love for you a hundred miles away."

My eyes started to water. What a life I had had! I

couldn't say anything. He went on…

"But, Adam, as far as your mother is concerned he told me nada. Niente. I asked him about it once or twice. I don't remember exactly what he said, but it was something like, 'She left the world…or disappeared…shortly after Adam was born…" I assumed she had died, but it was obvious that it was something he didn't want to talk about. Hence, I never pushed him on it. Like all good clowns, your father was a joker on the outside, but on the inside he was as serious as death. He just couldn't – or didn't want to – talk about it."

We both sipped some wine and I said, "That's pretty much what Peter Pittet said, too. I talked to him a few days ago."

"You know, Adam, I respect somebody's right not to talk about something. Everybody lives with his or her secrets. Unless we're talking about a crime, if people want to keep quiet about something, that's their business. The least we can do is respect the right to privacy about certain things. Friends are there to share things with, but they're also there to leave us alone when necessary."

"Of course."

"I'm sure Charley had his reasons for not talking about your mother. My guess is there was some deep hurt in there somewhere. And your father never wanted pain to be the focus of life, at least not overtly."

"Maybe I should just be happy to have been born and not worry about it anymore," I said.

"Adam, it's only normal that you to want to know who your mother is…or was. We all want to know where we came from. But you know, in the end, there are a lot more mysteries in this world than there are certainties. Maybe your mother will forever be one of those mysteries."

The food came and Danny Davenport and I talked about various things. Even his ex-wife…

"Did your father ever tell you what my ex-wife did to me?"

"Not that I know of. Do you have children?"

"One ex-wife, two kids. Let me tell you what this ex-femme of mine did. When my son – my youngest – turned eighteen, I flew with him to New York to help him get settled to start school at Columbia University. My daughter was already away in Chicago. I stayed with him for a week, and then flew home to Geneva. When I opened the door to our apartment, the place was completely empty except for my things. Absolutely everything was gone, except the bed, my clothes, books, desk, and my toiletries. In the bedroom there was a note on the pillow saying, 'I've waited for this moment for twenty years. Goodbye.' That was all. And I've never seen her since."

"Wow," was all I could think to say.

"Now I might not have been the best husband, but I'm not sure I deserved that. Imagine spending twenty-one years of your life with someone and having them tell you twenty of them were hell. Sometimes I wondered if my two children would have been better off with just one parent…like you. I tried to imagine the shock for them."

"Are they both okay now?"

"Yes, they seem to be. But one never knows what scars get left on minds and bodies. Life is never really what we think it is. Maybe that's a good lesson for everybody to learn at one time or another."

I couldn't disagree. And to think this man, Mr. Daniel Davenport, had been a professor of moral philosophy. Had he taught people what the good was? Or had he believed that there was no such thing as "the good", but only my good and your good? Anyway, as I drove home, I wondered how his mind had filed away those twenty-one years of living with a woman who didn't love him. Maybe that was why he dressed so dapperly – chaos on the inside, order on the outside.

One thing was certain: I had stopped feeling sorry for myself.

14

Peter Pittet is dead. He died humping. He died a soldier's death. Honorable. Died in combat. In love. Man versus the world. Man in the world. In search of… He wrote. He drank. He humped. His way of dealing with life. Of getting from one end to the other. As well as possible. Isn't that what we all do? Some have more luck than others. Or do it better. Though as I learned from Danny Davenport, it's hard to know who's really on top and who's on the bottom.

Pittet didn't quite make it until Christmas. Almost. The nineteenth of December was his last day. He left the newspaper building at around six. Slipped into the Café Lorado for a Pastis and a cigarette. Went to pick up his secretary at her apartment in Ouchy. They had made peace. Peace on earth. Good will toward women. He took her out to dinner at the Grappe d'Or. He knew the chef who knew what he liked, and the waiters who knew when to bring what to their table, always near the chimney with the orange lamp and the yellow roses and the huddle of glasses for the wine and water, the knives and forks lined three deep right and left for the scampi, turbot, and finally the lamb. It was his favorite restaurant on earth. He and she loved lamb and the chef knew how to make it taste almost like a dessert. After the lamb came another knife and fork for the cheese platter with three sorts of bread and a second bottle of red wine. A half hour later, the real desserts appeared, three shelves of them on a rolling chariot. Even though Peter Pittet wasn't a real dessert guy, he tried four that night, all wonderful (a light and dark chocolate mousse, a lemon tart, and a mille feuilles made with miniature raspberries). Cognac followed and Peter Baermann, the chef, came to their table. They talked about how good everything was. She said it was the best meal she'd ever had in her life not knowing his would end two hours later. They had coffee and the little cookies and chocolates that always came with it. At midnight the feast was over. Pittet and his girlfriend were the last customers to leave.

Baermann and his wife (the hostess) stood at the door and waved goodbye. Everyone said "Merry Christmas".

As they walked up the cobblestones of the Rue Cheneau de Bourg, Pittet gave the car keys to his girlfriend. He was staggering and knew enough to know that he shouldn't drive. They went to her second-floor apartment down by the lake. As they mounted the stairs he grabbed her enormous butt. Inside they hurried out of their clothes. When the ambulance guys got there he was already dead. They said it was certainly either a heart attack or a stroke and that this kind of thing happened more often than people thought. Her sobs hadn't silenced when they wheeled him out into the hall on the metal stretcher. The neighbors in the hall in their bathrobes watched as they carried him down the stairs. It was an old building and had no elevator.

The funeral was the day before Christmas. I went alone. I'm glad neither Pittet nor my father was there to see it. Had they been, they might have walked out when the priest said for the third time that the defunct was already reunited with his Maker and how lucky we all were that Jesus had died for our countless sins. Obviously Pittet hadn't had time to choreograph his last rites.

When we finally all filed out of the building, row-by-row, past the family, and into a little plaza at the Montoie cemetery, I saw Danny Davenport standing alone in the crowd outside. There had been a closing announcement saying there was a get together at a café down the street. We talked for a while comparing Dad's and Pittet's funeral. Eventually I excused myself saying I had to get home to put a turkey in the oven and the dogs in the garden. The second part wasn't true because my girlfriend was home to let out the dogs. It was true that I was the one who did the Christmas Eve turkey and my girlfriend would be waiting.

As I zigzagged through the crowd toward the parking lot, a woman in a brown hat and long brown coat stopped me and said, "Hello Adam. I thought I might see you here. It seems like every time I come to Lausanne now I end up at a funeral." It took a moment to figure out who was talking to me. When she asked if I got her note saying she'd be here for Christmas, I realized it was Lou-Lou, the woman from Paris that I'd met at Dad's funeral.

"Yes, I did," I said with a slight stumble. "It must have been about a month ago."

"I arrived here yesterday to spend Christmas with my father. Every year I think it could be our last together and every year here I am again. He's eighty-eight and probably doesn't care or know if it's Christmas, Valentine's Day, or the Marquis de Sade's birthday. But I come anyway. He is my father."

"Did you know Mr. Pittet well?" I asked.

"No, but I liked him at your father's funeral and when I'm here in Lausanne I always read the newspaper. He and your father were unique as far as sports columnists go. Sports were just a pretext for them to laugh at the world. Are you going to the café now?"

I explained I had to get home for Christmas Eve with my girlfriend. She said she had to go see her father in the rest home. She asked if she could call me in a couple of days. I looked forward to seeing her.

As I was driving home, I realized I hadn't seen Barbara Chardon at the funeral. Maybe she hadn't got word of Pittet's death. Maybe she had gone away for Christmas. Maybe Charley Lamb's funeral had been enough and she didn't want to truck with death for a while. Or who knows, maybe she didn't want to run into my girlfriend and me? Then again, perhaps she was there and I simply hadn't seen her.

I got to our quaint street a little after three. The air was a moist grey swirl that looked like it had just rolled in off an ocean. The dogs were yapping in the garden and my girlfriend was watching a film on television. I immediately went to work on the turkey. By four-fifteen it was in the oven. I realized we had no more bread, so decided I'd kill two birds with one stone. I loaded the dogs in the car and headed up to Denens, first for the bread, then for a dog-walk in the empty fields behind the village.

The shop in Denens is part of a dying species, a family business (bakery and a few grocery necessities) that is being suffocated by big supermarkets, even in Switzerland where traditions run deep and tend to hold firm. I patronize Mr. and Mrs. Beronie as often as possible to help them stay afloat. He's the baker and she runs the store. They decorate their front window for every holiday season. They know their clients by name. They always say hello, how are you, and goodbye. They seem to actually care about you and, who knows, they might, and you might care about them. They have a coffee machine in the corner and three stools so their customers can hang around for a bit.

I park next to a big Christmas tree decorated with ribbons and red lights. The store window is lit up and decorated with a homemade nativity scene that was probably the work of the Beronie kids. It is hard to tell

Joseph and Mary from the wise men. The barn is made of matches and popsicle sticks. The manger drowns in hay and angel hair hangs pell-mell from the stable rafters. I open the door and bells jingle.

"Nice decorations, Madame Beronie." She is rearranging what is left of the Christmas desserts.

"Thank you, Monsieur Lamb," she says. She keeps everybody on a surname basis. "We were a little late getting the decorations and things up this year."

"They're always nice."

"What brings you up here on Christmas Eve?"

"Bread and the dogs. But I think I'll have a cup of coffee." She hands me a jeton for the machine. "How much?" I ask.

"It's on Santa Claus," she says. "Speak of the devil. Here he is now." Her husband comes in through the back door from his ovens. He has a buche de Noël in each hand. The Beronies are one of those diametrical couples: she is tall and fleshy and he is short and skeletal. She looks like she would win the wrestling match, though they don't act like they're fighting types.

"Hi Mr. Beronie. Thanks for the coffee." I sit down on a stool. "Are you staying around for the holidays?"

"We're open until New Year's, then we're going to take the kids skiing. What about you and the missus?"

"We'll be here most of the time." The bell on the door jingles and in walks somebody I sense I have seen before. She has on a winter bonnet. When she pulls it off, she gives herself away: the Louise Brooks haircut. It is the young nurse from the Morges hospital, my father's last object of desire, the final dish on Charley Lamb's long and winding menu. I sit there like a dummy and for an instant I feel a combination of great joy and a desire to cry. The world was too wonderful and too sad. Dad and Pittet dead. This beautiful young woman is standing there. The kindness of the Beronies. The warmth of the little shop on Christmas Eve. I watch the nurse ask for "une bagette and une buche de Noël". I'm not sure if I will say anything to her. If she doesn't look at me I probably won't; if she does I'm quite sure I will. She stands waiting in front of the counter as Mrs. Beronie sets the cake inside a box and folds the sides up. She looks in her handbag for her wallet and then turns and glances my way. She smiles. I can't resist.

"Bonjour," I say.

"Bonjour," she answers with an I-know-you-from-somewhere look of her own on her lovely face.

After a short hesitation, I say, "Yes, I think we know each other...My father's funeral. He was the one who...who..."

"Who what?" Mrs. Beronie says as she put the box on the counter. She had met my dad a few times.

"Who...who...appreciated what a wonderful nurse he had before he died. Mademoiselle is a nurse," I say to Madame Beronie. Then to her, "I'm sorry, but I forget your name."

"Actually I don't think I ever officially introduced myself."

"Maybe you didn't."

"You're Adam. I remember your name because there aren't many Adams around anymore. There are more Eves than Adams these days. I'm not Eve. But I'm close. Ava. My father loved the actress Ava Gardner. I'm Ava Margot."

"Do you live near here?" I ask.

"Up the street in the next village. In Bussy-Chardonney. Where do you live, Adam?"

"In Morges, near the Interio furniture store." We were talking about twenty feet from each other. I got off my stool and asked her if I could buy her a cup of coffee.

"I normally don't drink coffee after the sun goes down, but since there hasn't been any sun today, pourquoi pas?"

I arrange a stool a few feet across from me. She pays Madame Beronie for the cake, then comes over and sits down. Madame Beronie smiles and gives me another slug for the coffee machine.

"I would have liked to have stayed longer after your father's funeral, but I had to work," she says lifting her coffee toward her lips and her eyes toward me.

"We had a good time. Almost too good. Some of us almost didn't make it home. But I'm sure that's how my father would have wanted it."

"You know, I've thought about him quite a few times since he died." She pivots on the stool and crosses her legs. "I think I was the last person he talked to. In fact I know I was because I was the only nurse on the floor the night he passed away. It's kind of a funny feeling."

Passed way away, I think. "He must have liked you, Ava," I say thinking how we all like to hear our names. "He was actually quite picky about who he tried to put his paws on." We both laugh.

"The night he died – I mean the night before the morning he died – we talked quite a bit. He'd find excuses to ring his bell. There weren't many patients on the floor and I enjoyed talking to him. He said some interesting things. Most people get sentimental and nostalgic before they die. He acted like the party was just getting started."

"Maybe he didn't know he was going to die…. In

any case, I'm glad it's not just his aggressive side that you remember."

"He wasn't aggressive. That's just it. He was as gentle as a kitten. He just wanted to touch me."

I have nothing to lose, so I tell the truth. "Ava, I'll be honest with you…. He loved the human body. Some bodies more than others, of course. But he loved to touch people he liked. Too much I guess. It used to get him into trouble sometimes."

"I remember one thing in particular he said…something about how men and women today have forgotten that they're nature's opposites and that their difference is what is beautiful…and what makes the world go round. He said all this sexist business had turned everything into a nasty struggle for power and love these days had lost its luster."

"It's amazing he was talking about that just before he died. But yes, love and power were two of his favorite subjects." I suddenly realized this was the first time since he died that I could talk about him without getting emotional. I guess that was a good sign. "I'm glad he had you to talk to…I wish I'd been there."

"Of course. I don't think anybody knew he would go that fast. The doctors hadn't even talked about putting him in Intensive Care." She re-crossed her legs. "I did think something might be up when he asked me for a piece of paper, but he said he was just writing something down he didn't want to forget."

All this time Mrs. Beronie is pretending she isn't listening, but she is. She takes a couple of steps toward us and asks if we want a little chocolate to go with the coffee. I decline saying it would spoil my appetite for the turkey, but Ava takes a truffle.

I need to go. "Listen, I'd better get moving. I've got two dogs in the car waiting for their last walk before it gets dark."

Ava says, "I just want you to know that your father was the first patient whose funeral I went to without really knowing anybody in the family."

"We're both honored. Thanks."

"It was as if I wanted to talk with him one last time. I was kind of curious to see who his friends and family were, too."

"He didn't have too many friends as you might have noticed."

"Yeah," she said. "It surprised me. Then again it didn't. He said more than once that he rarely met people who realized how incredible life was. That was another thing I remembered. He said nothing bored him more than people who thought they knew what existence was all about. He told me he loved the world, but was a bit tired of living in it."

There is a moment of silence. I thank her again for keeping my father company, and add, "Ava, I think you were a perfect last person for him to have talked to."

She smiles (O beauty!) and says, "I'd better be going too. My boyfriend's parents are coming over. I just came up for the dessert. He's going to think I crashed in the fog." She gathers her things and we walk to the door together.

"It is foggy out there. Be careful. Maybe we'll meet another time."

"Merry Christmas," she says.

"Same to you."

She leans forward and gives me the Swiss three-kiss routine. I want to grab her. I'm not Charley Lamb's son for nothing. But of course I don't.

PART III

15

What I've always noticed about Christmas is how fast it goes. You do all the planning, shopping, and decorations like it's going to last forever. But it doesn't. It's over before you can say, "c'est la vie". I continue to celebrate it because my father and I always did, in spite of the fact that he didn't believe in much of anything. He liked the music, the lights, the tree in the house, the presents, and he liked to cook. We never did Thanksgiving. He said that after what "Americans" did to the "Indians", he couldn't see any point in the tradition. But we never missed a Christmas. He liked the idea that there once lived a kind gentle man named Jesus. It was always just the two of us. Sometimes he'd invite the neighbors over for a drink in the afternoon. But otherwise it was just father and son. He didn't spoil me with an excess of presents, but he wasn't ungenerous either. He believed the giver had the most fun, but in our case I think it was pretty even. He usually gave me things we could play with or build together, like Lego, model planes, and Monopoly. I think my favorite present came in a huge box when I was five or six. It was a mass of wooden blocks he had cut and painted himself in all different shapes and colors. We built houses, chateaux, cities, bridges, airports, and skyscrapers. Things always had animal names, some in French, some in English: a house was "La Maison du Gentil Chien"; a bridge called "Pont Penguin"; an airport was "J.F. Kittycat"; we named a skyscraper "La Tour de Giraffe". I must have played with these blocks until I was twelve.

One Christmas we flew to America and spent the holiday at his brother's house in California just outside of Sacramento. The brother was a few years older than my father, and his kids were older than me. They said prayers before meals and had pictures of Jesus all over the place. On Christmas Eve they told stories about Bethlehem and Jerusalem and recited passages from the Bible. His wife played organ music. Everybody was nice, but for some reason, it just didn't feel like Christmas. We didn't go back.

I never saw my grandparents. My father's father died of a heart attack shortly after he – my father – came to Europe and long before I was born. The story I got was that my grandfather, Jack Lamb, was quietly having breakfast one spring morning in sunny California. He suddenly heard a loud crash outside. He put down his spoon and newspaper, got up from the table, and ran up the street toward the noise. He didn't make it to the scene. He fell over dead trying to help two sixteen-year-olds who were driving their parents' second cars to high school. A girl had been backing out of her driveway. A boy was changing channels on the radio and didn't see the other car's big rear slide into the street. The kids weren't hurt, but my grandfather died.

I do remember that when I was five or six we had planned to go spend Christmas with my grandmother who still lived in the family house in Piedmont, California. But that autumn she got some kind of nasty flu and died before we got on the plane. We were able to change the tickets to go to her funeral. All I remember was that the coffin was a pinkish color and the church smelled like a flower shop.

Today is December twenty-seventh. My girlfriend

left this morning to go see her parents in Fribourg. In the past, we invited them and my father for Christmas Day, but her father just had something taken out of his insides, so they didn't come down this year. It's just as well. She and I hit kind of a low point after the turkey dinner on the twenty-fourth. The meal was delicious and I had brought out my best bottle of Bourgogne, a 1982 Gevrey-Chambertin. I had made a fire in the chimney and Placido Domingo was singing carols. After dinner we gave each other presents. Then all I wanted to do was make love. A good meal and Christmas music does that to me. But for whatever reason, she wanted no part of it. She wanted to watch TV. I went for a walk, came back, and she was still watching TV. I went to bed sensing something was askew in paradise. I imagine she did, too. The twenty-fifth I went skiing by myself in Leysin. Yesterday the only words we exchanged were about what we were going to have for dinner. I almost went skiing again today, but when I got up it looked like it was going to snow. I love skiing on the stuff, but I hate driving on it.

An hour ago the phone rang. It was Lou-Lou, Dad's first European girlfriend. She invited me for a drink at the famous Beau Rivage Hotel in Lausanne where she was staying. Elizabeth Taylor and Richard Burton were said to have periodically holed up there between divorces for a few days of eating, drinking, fighting, and screwing. The place has the best Christmas lights in the city. It really is — as it calls itself — one of the world's finest hotels. She suggested we meet in the English bar and asked me what would be a good time. I don't know why I said five, because I've got nothing to do all day: I've finished my translations; my girlfriend's in Fribourg; the dogs have been walked; I've done the dishes and even vacuumed the living room. Anyway, five it was.

I thought about calling Barbara Chardon. Ten minutes later I really thought about calling Barbara Chardon. Five minutes later I called Barbara Chardon. She wasn't home.

I read the newspaper for a while. Then I thought about calling Ava Margot. But Ava Margot lived with her boyfriend (Barbara Chardon lived with herself). If anything was to happen with Ava Margot, the universe would have to grind its gears and produce a massive matrix of circumstances, e.g. Ava Margot and her boyfriend have a fight; my girlfriend and I continue having a cold war; Ava parks her car here at 3:13 one day; I park my car there at 3:16 on the same day; we both walk toward our respective destinations; our paths cross at 3:19; after I go to the post office and she goes to the bank we both have time to meet for a coffee; we go to a pleasant tea-room and everything is as pleasant as two puppies meeting on a sandy beach; I ask her how her boyfriend is; she says they broke up last week; I say that's too bad meaning it's too good; she is free to accept my invitation for pizza the next night; the pizza rendezvous goes wonderfully well; we have not only my father in common but other things like a love for Venice and walking in the mountains and Tchaikovsky's fourth, fifth, and sixth symphonies; we share a bottle of Chianti; we go back to her apartment in Bussy-Chardonney, we have a glass of Remy Martin; we make love once on the living room floor; I look into her cocoa eyes and see joy; she never acts like she is performing; she doesn't scramble to put her clothes back on, nor does she make an effort to flaunt her natural jewels; we relax; she invites me to sleep there; we share her tooth brush; she smells like heaven and I like to lick heaven; we make more than love; we fall asleep; around six a.m. a leg stirs then two legs stir, then four, and Adam's cane is steel and Ava's valley is moist; this Black and Decker is for Ava Margot and only Ava Margot; she loves it; I love it; Charley Lamb's vision of man and woman is not a damp dream, but the most tangible thing on this earth.... Aren't all amorous encounters an incredible series of coincidences?

It's now three o'clock. I pet the dogs' heads for a while. I turn a few more pages of the newspaper. I turn the TV on and off. I think about calling Barbara Chardon again. I call Barbara Chardon again. Seven dead rings in a lonely cave. I feed the dogs. I listen to Tchaikovsky's 1812 Overture, Opus 49. I wish somebody would tell me what the hell "opus" means. Why don't painters have "opuses"? Or poets? I should look it up. I will look it up. I do look it up. Webster says…"Opus, a creative work; especially a musical composition. Used with a number to designate the order of a composer's work." And to think that for all these years I thought opus meant something exciting, something profound, something that could only be understood by great musical minds. But no. Just a work with a number attached to it, like Barry Bonds' 73rd home run. It should be called, "Bonds, Opus 73." Sounds sexier. Would make baseball look more intellectual.

I am waiting for five o'clock, trying to kick time – like a bent can – down the road. I've got another hour. I decide to go up to the attic and have a look at the Chiquita banana boxes. Maybe I'll uncover some new archaeological Charley Lamb relics. Amazingly I do.

In the second box I dig through, I find a handwritten story he wrote in 1980 that, for some reason, I haven't read. Attached to it is a letter to Playboy magazine. Did he ever send it off? Did it ever get published? Did it come back rejected? I don't know. I spread out on the floor and read it. Two curious coincidences strike me cold: the title, "The Eiffel Tower", I have used as a label for one of my ten erection categories; the heroine is a nurse like Ava Margot. How much of the story is based on fact, I have no idea.

THE EIFFEL TOWER

by Charles Lamb

"When we finish," Johnson said pulling back his head for a little air, "I'll tell you what it's like to have the Eiffel Tower in your mouth."

Karen laughed in the semi-dark and reset her center on his face. Seek my face, he thought. Childbirth was now in the past. So was the dripping, swelling, cupping, and bottle saving of breast-feeding. The baby was asleep in the room next to theirs with eight months of life under its –

his – belt. There was space anew for Johnson, there was a place in Karen's life for her husband's vital shenanigans. Vital he now knew because he had been close to crazy for the first seven months after the baby had been born. Karen had kept saying no, no, not now, and dreams of ex-girlfriends, hookers, belly dancers, sheep, goats, Mimi of "La Bohème", neighbors, buxom acquaintances, and over-rated film stars had haunted Johnson's head like tumors. Abstinence had stretched from days into weeks into months and his forgotten organ had fought for survival like a headless worm on a rain-drenched sidewalk.

The elongated triangle again settled between his upper row of teeth and his tongue, that glorious pink slab of taste buds pasted microscopically to his mouth at conception. He often wondered where he'd be without it. When all else failed, his tongue was always there to give him a reason to be. When work was a bore he always knew he could come home to food and often enough to Karen's honeyed slit. One of the reasons he had married her was her taste, that is, how she tasted in his greedy mouth. During courtship she had always left him licking his slick lips as he would drive home in the early morning or the middle of the night. And work was often a bore, so Karen's cooking and sweet socket made many a day bearable. Johnson managed a discount shoe store in the mall on the outskirts of Sacramento, a job he fell into when he had nothing to do after graduating from UC Davis twenty years before. His degree in sociology was as useless as a discarded cheeseburger wrapper, so he had taken the first job he found that would pay his measly rent and feed his stomach. He had started at the bottom, but within three years had worked his way to manager because of his ability to calmly take crap from customers and listen to the babble of his superiors with a smile on his face. After studying the social sciences, Johnson didn't believe people were free; he saw them like clouds in the sky or weeds in his wild garden.

"Stop, stop," Karen said with muffled joy so as not to wake the baby. "It's too much."

"In this business too much is never enough," he said as he craned his neck for new air.

"You're crazy, honey," she said.

"Crazy does what crazy is," he piped. "I'm just trying to set the universe straight."

"Psss," she whispered, "you'll wake Sandy." Then she blurted out a few signs of satisfaction, hammered a couple fingernails into his shoulders, then slid back and mounted his throbbing staff. In turn, Johnson praised the world as he fired once, twice, thrice into the murky moist heavens, eventually pulling Karen to his horizontal side, and pulling the covers over his chilly legs. Emptied, he kissed her because he loved her.

That night Johnson dreamed that his mother told him that she loved every cell of her husband's body. Her husband was Johnson's father and his dead mother's words about his dead father were both stunning and soothing: stunning because she had been raised a Quaker and the body hadn't been her favorite subject, soothing because Johnson – on awaking – had taken it to mean that she had enjoyed being married to his father. They had always seemed to get along, but Johnson, from the day he himself had lived a real copulation, had always wondered how things had been for his parents. He knew that as his father had got older his faith in an afterlife had diminished and he had periodically hinted to Johnson that he had better get what he could while the restaurant was open. His mother, on the other hand, had talked more and more about heaven, as her rope got shorter. When his – Johnson's – high school years were drab, she would tell him not to worry, that this life was only a testing ground for an eternity in heaven. Johnson wasn't as sure as his mother seemed to be.

His father died the year before he got married and his mother followed six months later, as often happens with loving couples. Johnson was now forty-four and his wife thirty-five. He had married late, at forty-two, because deep in his heart he couldn't imagine anyone would want to be with him – or anyone else for that matter – longer than a few months. He and all the women he had known had tired of each other with the passing of a few seasons. Once, with Sherry Simon, he had made it from Thanksgiving to Thanksgiving, but by Christmas the only gift he wanted to give her was a one-way ticket out of his life and all she gave him were the keys to his apartment.

When his parents died, however, he took out a new lease on life, or rather life took out a new lease on him. He had no brothers and sisters and the world had suddenly become too barren. An aunt in Chicago, an uncle in Tampa, and a couple of cousins thousands of miles away were not enough to keep him feeling at home on a world map. Plus, he had met Karen – she was a nurse at the hospital where his mother perished – and she was the finest flavor on the Baskin-Robbins menu. Now he wanted to reproduce and so did she. Her boyfriend prior to him had been as sterile as a dentist's office; she was ready for the brazen bull. Johnson threw away his prophylactics and she was pregnant within a week. They got married a month later in an A-frame church in Lake Tahoe, honeymooned in Harrah's south shore, moved into a condo ten minutes from the mall, waited out the human gestation period with reasonable success, and now were three.

"So what does the Eiffel Tower feel like in your mouth?" she said as she flipped out the light and came back to bed in her white cotton nightgown.

"Like an extra tooth."

"It does not."

"How would you know?"

"I wouldn't, but I know it's a lot softer than a tooth."

"You're right. It's more like one of those granular corn candies we used to get as kids that melt in your mouth."

"But it doesn't melt."

"You're right again. Okay, it's like a piece of rubber that you'd bite off of the inside of an old tennis ball."

"You're terrible."

"I'm trying to tell you something – something important."

"Then tell me, you babbling bubble gum machine."

"That's it, it's like bubble gum, old hard bubble gum. The difference is that when you put old hard bubble gum in your mouth, it gets softer, but with this, the real Eiffel Tower, the longer it stays in your mouth the harder it gets."

"Very abstruse."

"Okay. What it's really like is if you take one of those rubbery grey-brown mushrooms you find floating in Chinese fish soup and fold it and pack it together. That's it. That's it, that is, if you then leave just a bit of the fish soup smell on the warm amorphous wad and then coat it with a thin layer of the finest honey bees can buy, then you have it in all its splendor."

"You're nuts."

"My true nature revealed. Thank you, darling."

Karen fell asleep before her husband did, but it was she who would rise first before the day's light to the sweet snarl of their living baby. Johnson, as he drifted off, wondered how many bulls on the ranch truly marveled at nature's multifarious architectural miracles.

When I finished the story I thought, *Charley Lamb really was a lover of life.* And here he had torn me out of my boredom. (How can one be bored in such an incredible world?) In the story there was a father, a mother, a baby (me?), dead parents, and a lot of my father's talk about life. I don't know how I had missed it when I cleaned out his apartment. What facts were floating in the fiction? Would I ever know? I liked the last line about the bulls appreciating nature's wonders.

I looked at the clock. It was four-thirty. Time to go to the Hotel Beau Rivage.

16

I thought I was early, but when I walked in Lou-Lou was already there, in a high chair at the end of the bar, sipping a drink through a straw. She was wearing a black dress with a scarlet scarf neatly arranged around her neck. She saw me, smiled, and fluttered her fingers. We exchanged the three kisses. She picked up her glass and we went to a small couch near the window. Not far from us were a silent piano and a large Christmas tree decorated with turtledoves and gold balls. An elderly couple and the bartender were the only other people in the room.

"How was Christmas?" she asked.

"Well, it was my first one without my father.

Normally my girlfriend's parents come down from Fribourg, but they couldn't make it this year because her father just had an operation. It was only the two of us. A little quiet." I didn't go into details. "And yours? How's your father?"

"Alive. I think I told you he's eighty-eight. He seems to be holding on to life like a young child holds on to a favorite rag or ragdoll. I finally had to put him in a home last year, so we celebrated with all his buddies and the local staff. It was actually quite amusing. Before we opened the presents, the staff tried to get everybody to sing Christmas carols. It was like the tower of Babel on an animal farm. Later, when they opened their presents, it seemed like the real pleasure was taking off the wrapping paper. Most of them would stare rather blankly at what was inside. It was a new kind of Christmas. My father doesn't talk much anymore, but he smiles a lot."

The waiter came in his bow tie and plaid vest. I ordered a small bottle of white wine. As we waited for my drink, Lou-Lou said, "I decided to treat myself to a week in this hotel. Being from Lausanne, I'd never stayed here before, and with my father no longer in his apartment, I decided to 'me dorloter', as we say in French." It was interesting that we were speaking in English. For some reason it was our chosen common language from the first time we talked after Charley Lamb's funeral.

"How are the rooms?" I asked.

"Like you'd expect. And the service is wonderful. I sleep like a baby."

"You haven't told me what took you to Paris?"

"Well, it's a long story. You could say I wanted a change from Lausanne, and the big city lights. I've been there for almost forty years. At first, I studied at the Sorbonne...English literature in fact. Suddenly, I decided I wanted to be an actress. While I was trying to be an actress I worked in bars and restaurants to pay the rent." The waiter came with the wine, a bowl of olives, and a pile of mixed nuts. We thanked him and Lou-Lou went on. "Then, when I finally did get to be an actress I still had to work in bars and restaurants to pay the bills. I jumped around from TV junk to B movies. I even did a couple of take-off-your-clothes movies. Did you ever see 'Emmanuelle', that soft porn flick that took Europe by storm about thirty years ago? I had a small part in that. It was a lousy film but it sold tickets. All the while I tried to write a novel that never got published. I even taught English for a while. The last ten years I've been working for a perfume company. What about yourself, Adam? What fills up your time?"

I grabbed some olives and took a sip of my wine. The more I knew about Lou-Lou, the more I wanted to know. "My life isn't as exciting as yours..."

"Don't be so sure about that," she interrupted. "Movie-making is one of the most over-rated activities on the planet. A hundred years from now history is going to look back at the 'star system' we have today and laugh its head off. Most of the 'stars' I met were no more interesting than the postman or the ice cream vendor. Often less, in fact. But that's another story. What do you do?"

"I make my living as a translator. It's rather boring, but it does give me a lot of free time."

"And what do you do in your free time?"

"Good question…. I walk dogs. Wander around. Wander around some more. Walk dogs again. I do listen to music a lot."

"How many dogs? Your dogs?"

"Yeah, ours. Two. Big dogs that need a lot of walking. I'd say I need a lot of walking, too."

"And the music... Do you play music, too?"

"No, I don't. I've got a lousy ear. Good enough for listening maybe, but bad for playing."

"One doesn't know until one tries." Lou-Lou smiled, delicately sucked on her straw, and looked around the room. I looked at her. I can't remember ever feeling so at ease with somebody after such a short time. She was as relaxed as a teddy bear and always seemed happy to be where she was. She had a charm that was hard to define. It started with her feet and moved up her body like a spider up a wall. The more we talked the lovelier she became.

"Do you have any children?" she asked looking back at me.

"No. I'm forty years old and figure I've still got time. To be honest, it's not the kids I worry about – it's wondering if I want to stay with the same woman long enough to raise the kids. I've noticed that after a few years with somebody things have a tendency to change for the worse – at least from the man's point of view, if you know what I mean."

"Of course. But don't think they don't change for the woman, too. They just change in different ways."

"Yes, I'm sure they do. What about you? Do you have children?"

"One from a first marriage. One from a second marriage. And one from no marriage."

"Are they all grown?"

"All are out of the house at least. They all seem to be doing well enough."

The waiter came by to be sure everything was okay. Lou-Lou ordered another cocktail, then changed her mind and said she'd have some white wine with me. I asked for another half bottle.

"Did you act in any other films I might know about?" I asked.

"If you looked hard enough, you could see me lying around a swimming pool or two in some of the follow-up 'Emmanuelle' films. I was also in one with Jean-Paul Belmondo called 'Le Professionnel'. But I didn't have a major part."

"I might have seen that," I said.

"If you didn't, you didn't miss anything. It was about a hired killer who was supposed to assassinate an African president. One of those 'waste-two-hours-rather-rapidly' thriller movies."

For a quick second I looked at her eyes. They reminded me of Ava Margot's. They were not big, but the shape was a delicate oblong with lovely edges. "Did you ever do any modeling?" I asked, not necessarily to flatter her.

"For about twenty minutes, thirty years ago. Not only did you have to sleep with people to get anywhere, but you had to make them feel like they were important. I thought I could make a few quick francs, but it wasn't worth the time I was wasting. Unfortunately, my first husband was a photographer I met in those twenty minutes. We stayed together long enough to make a cute little girl, but not long enough to raise her together past the age of three. I think his camera was like an extra hand to take women's clothes off. In the end I didn't really mind because I realized I didn't love him…and the feeling was probably reciprocal. You've never been married, Adam?"

"No. To be honest, I often wonder if any man should get married. Aren't we all pigs? Aren't we all like that first husband of yours?"

"I've often wondered. But I did have a lover once who swore to me that when he truly loved a woman he had absolutely no desire to sleep with – or even touch – anybody else. He said he thought most men simply didn't profoundly love the person they were being unfaithful to. Maybe he was right. I can't imagine Romeo cheating on Juliet. Can you?"

"No…not really."

"Well, that's what he meant. He said I was his Juliet and he had no desire for another woman. I was deeply touched."

"So what happened?"

"We eventually broke up."

"Why?"

"I was young. Too young. Too young to know what real love was."

"Do you know now?"

"I'm not sure. I'm not sure about a lot of things."

We were silent for a while. The piano started playing. I couldn't believe how comfortable it was sitting with her. I finally said, "Do you like living in Paris?"

"It has its plusses and minuses. I love the architecture and all the old neighborhoods. But getting around can be rather cumbersome. I live next to a little park in the Marais, not far from the Picasso museum. I walk to and from work, but otherwise I don't go out much anymore."

"I love Paris. Actually I love all big European cities…If you don't mind my asking, what happened with your second husband?"

"He was Irish, from Dublin. Quite a guy. A writer and a good one. Unfortunately he didn't have the success Joyce had. He was teaching English at the same school I was in Paris. We stayed together long enough to have a son and then raise the son and my daughter together for a few years. But he smoked too many cigarettes. Those nasty yellow ones with no filter. He died of lung cancer when he was fifty-five. I was quite a bit younger."

"I'm sorry…"

"Don't be sorry. It was his fault. But he was a very good teacher…and father for that matter. He loved the English language and passed that love on to his students.”

“Didn’t you say you met my father when he was teaching?”

“Yes, I think I did. But I was a student, not a colleague. Actually my second husband reminded me a little of your father. He was also quite a bit older than I was. And, like Charley, he had the same relaxed style about everything – like underwear. He wore loose underwear. All the French were cutting off their circulation with their bikini briefs.” She smiled. “I don’t know why I’m telling you all this…”

“I know why, because I’m enjoying it,” I said flippantly.

“Well good, because I’m enjoying telling you. I really don’t have a lot of people I talk to these days. My children have been gone for a few years. Ralph – my second husband – and I did have quite a bit of fun together. He never took anything too seriously, except life itself. Everything and nothing was sacred to him.”

“I’d say that’s the way my father was, too.”

“I’d agree. Like I said, there were similarities.”

“Where are your children now?”

“My son lives outside of Boston. He went to school there and ended up staying. He has a good job with Staples, that big office supply company. It’s funny how children go their own way. Neither my husband nor I had any interest in business."

"Did I tell you that I went to school in Arizona?"

"I don't think so."

"I loved the desert and the weather. I don't really know why I came back. I guess it was to be with my father."

"That wouldn't have been a bad reason. There are lots of good things here in Switzerland and your father was one of them." I watched her hand rise, float down, and land on my knee. "Adam, are you hungry? Can I invite you to dinner? They have a wonderful restaurant downstairs, the 'Café Beau Rivage'."

"I should be the one taking you out. You've come all the way from Paris."

"I'm the one staying in the fancy hotel. It's my week for splurging. It's on me. It's a little early. What time is it? A little after six I think? They start serving dinner at seven." She paused. Her hand had left my knee. "Look, why don't you come up to my room for few minutes? You can see how the 'other half' lives. Then we can eat downstairs. You're not in a hurry, are you?"

"No, not at all."

As we finished the wine, she told me a story about when she and my father were hiking in the mountains, got caught in a huge thunderstorm, and found refuge with a peasant family in an "alpage". She said they were some of the nicest, most unforgettable people she had ever met in her life. She and my father ended up sleeping in the barn with the cows. She said, "Adam, your father used to have a theory about hotels… 'The number of orgasms you have in a hotel is inversely proportional to the number of stars on the sign out front.'"

We both laughed. I called the waiter and paid the bill. As the piano player went into a jazzy rendition of White Christmas, Lou-Lou took my elbow and guided me out of the bar toward the elevator.

17

When we stepped inside she was still holding my arm. "Push four," she said. I saw the back of her head and neck in the mirror. I again wondered how old she was. The first time I saw her I had thought she might be close to sixty because she had said something about being more than a decade younger than my father. In the twilight of the bar she could have been forty-five. As we stood in the elevator she could have been thirty-nine. Did it matter? No. She was lovely. I tried to think if there was an opposite to the expression "robbing the cradle"… "Crackin' the coffin" maybe?

The elevator door opened. We turned left and her room was the first one we came to. She fumbled in her purse for her plastic key. I looked down at her neck and wanted to kiss it. The door clicked open and Lou-Lou stepped inside flicking on the light. Somebody who loved the color salmon had decorated the room. There was a huge bed with a beautiful apricot bedspread. The carpet reminded me of coral. The bedside lamps were gold with titian shades. Across from the bed was a huge antique armoire that probably hid a television. Between that and a Louis XVI desk was a mini bar. A love seat and a round table beckoned near the window. Without a word, Lou-Lou knelt down and opened the mini bar. Then she turned, looked halfway up to my head, and suggested a small bottle of rosé champagne. "I haven't been able to drink the stuff alone," she said.

"Fine," I said. "The room is lovely."

She handed me the bottle and as I began unpeeling the top wrapper I walked across the room and looked out the window. She had a vast southerly view and I could see the lights of Evian across the lake in France. A few snowflakes were falling. Lou-Lou set two glasses on the table while I uncorked the bottle. She took her glass and sat on the bed cross-legged. I dropped onto the love seat.

We exchanged "santés", our glasses clicked and our eyes met. She took a small sip, then said, "Adam, I need to tell you something." She looked at the bubbles rising in her glass, then back at me.

"Do you remember at the end of the party after your father's funeral when we walked back to his grave?"

"I was pretty drunk, but yeah, sure I do."

"Do you remember what I said?"

"I think you said something about how you had loved him."

"That's right. I said I loved him. Then I said your mother loved him, too. Adam, we're the same person."

18

I can't tell you everything about what happened after she told me. But I'll do the best I can. First, she cried a lot more than I did. I remember that as I sat there trembling, her glass fell on the table and she lunged onto the love seat and started kissing me. Her wet face slid back and forth on my cheeks. She said my name a couple of times, then she dropped to the ground and held my legs as if she were tackling me. I remember planting my fingers in her hair and rubbing her skull. I closed my eyes and had a vision of my father holding my hand as we crossed the road near Barbara Chardon's apartment to go to "our beach". That's when I started to cry. After a couple minutes she was still on her knees. I finally lifted her up to the love seat. We sat there for a good while without saying anything except "O Adam" and "O Mother" between deep breaths and sniffles. When we both got back a semblance of composure, she suddenly got up and went into the bathroom closing the door behind her. I recall thinking I had just seen one of the calmest, most composed women on earth completely lose control of herself. For me, it was as if forty years of absence were recouped in a matter of minutes. I had a mother.

I heard the shower go on. I poured the last of the champagne and went out on the balcony. A steady snowfall had started. I stood there until I was cold, then scurried back into the warmth of the room, took off my shoes, and lay down on the bed. Of course a million things were going through my head, but I was tired and so happy. I felt like I had run ten miles. Make that forty. But hey, I had a mother and she loved me. I won't bullshit you: it was better late than never. When she finally came out of the bathroom she was wearing different clothes. I remember the color was emerald green.

We went down to the restaurant. As dinner unfolded so did her story.... She was not quite eighteen when I was born. Her birthday was in May and I was born at the end of April. She had dropped out of school the second semester. Though she had feared childbirth, I actually came out rather smoothly. She was still living with her parents, so her father and mother had taken her to the hospital. They knew Charley Lamb and liked him very much. They had called him from the hospital. He was there a few minutes after I was born.

It turns out that Lou-Lou's parents were the ones who had given my father the okay to make love with her. Charley knew the Swiss law – between sixteen and eighteen only the girl's parents could file a complaint. Lou-Lou was seventeen and wasn't at Charley's school anymore. As long as her parents consented, she and my father could make all the love they wanted to. Which evidently was a whole lot. She said they must have made love a thousand times that first year together, and that I probably exist because of a busted prophylactic. Imagine owing your existence to a faulty condom…. I'm sure I'm hardly alone.

They thought about an abortion, but Lou-Lou was the one who said no. My father had said the final decision had to be hers. They had also considered giving me away for adoption. In fact, that had been more or less the plan – until my father held me in his arms. She said he said from that moment on it would have been impossible for him to give me away.

So what happened? Why had I ended up alone with Charley Lamb? Lou-Lou explained everything at our table that night in the Café Beau Rivage. She said the crazy thing was that she loved my father. But she knew at the time that she couldn't stay with him. She had to live her life. Something in her gut told her she had to be free. She gave life to the baby, but now she wanted the baby to give freedom to her. She and my father made an agreement: She would finish her school; when I was one year old, she would go Paris alone and live her dreams; I would live with my father; "But," my father said, "if you leave, it is for good…never ever come back." That was the deal. They both stuck to it. She said that her leaving absolutely shattered him. But he had me. I was his defense against a fractured heart – I and the guarantee that he would never see my beautiful mother again.

And she never came back…until he died.

Here she said that she had not told me the truth about one little detail: It wasn't by accident that she was in Lausanne for his funeral. For the past twenty years she had subscribed to the 24 Heures, the Lausanne newspaper that my father had a column in. She wanted to read his stuff and she wanted to follow the obituaries to know if and when he died…so she could come and see me. She told me this part of the story while we were eating dessert and the loveliest teardrops a child has ever seen were rolling down her cheeks onto her plate of white chocolate mousse. She said that when she read of my father's death she caught the first train to Lausanne. She also told me that the lover she had talked about – the one who had said he could not touch another woman when he was truly in love – was my father. Yes, the woman across the table was the only woman Charley Lamb had truly loved.

Before I accompanied her back up to her room, Lou-Lou reached across the table and took my hand. She said she had wondered a million times how our lives would have been had she stayed with my father and me. But of course no one would ever know.

POSTSCRIPT

The events of this story took place between October and December 2003. It is now almost a year later. Things have happened…

My girlfriend and I separated right after New Year's Day. On the night of the 31st all she wanted to do was to watch television again. That did it. She moved out the first week of 2004. The great cogwheels of the universe then took over. In February I met Ava Margot next to the fresh vegetable section in the Aldi supermarket in Morges. We finished our respective shopping and went for a drink by the lake. The next night we went out for a pizza. She was still living with her boyfriend, but the fuse had burned out, there was no more joy to their love, and she was only there until she could find her own place. She came to my house after dinner that night. She never did get her own apartment. In March she moved in with me. She likes the dogs and, as you can imagine, she's not the type to be bothered by the trains or the freeway. Adam's cane has never been so operative.

My mother has decided to move back to Lausanne in January of next year. One morning last April her father wandered away from his "home". Nobody really knows for how long he was gone or where he had been before he walked in front of a train. He had got to the town of Pully next to Lausanne. The guardrail was down and the red lights were flashing, but he simply slipped through the turnstile and wandered onto the tracks. The conductor told the police that the old man smiled and waved to him as he unsuccessfully slammed on the brakes. My mother was here for the funeral and that's when she told me she was moving back.

Danny Davenport called not long ago to invite me to his wedding. He had attended a banquet at the United Nations in Geneva and was seated next to "a beautiful blonde" who had just retired after working thirty-five years in the anti-land mine program. He said a couple mines blew up under their table and they've been together ever since. The wedding is set for the fourteenth of January.

I see Barbara Chardon quite frequently, though she doesn't see me. In September she started working as a weatherwoman for the Television Suisse Romande. Evidently, ever since she started doing the forecast at the end of the nightly news, audience ratings have never been so high.

I went to Jacques Bolle's wine shop last week to stock up for the holidays. We had a drink together and talked about my father, his wife's bad back, and the quality of this year's vintage. He said it would be an excellent year for both reds and whites.

The only news I have about Isabella, the Romanian singer, is from a newspaper ad I saw recently in the Journal de Morges. She's starting up her own music school for children right here in town. If our plans pan out, Ava Margot and I should have a couple of students for her before you can say "c'est la vie." At last report it looks like one might already be on the way…

The other night Ava told me a story about Charley Lamb when he was in the Morges hospital that she said she had never told anybody… "It was probably three days before he died. He knew I was on night duty. About four o'clock in the morning he rang his bell for assistance. When I came in the room to check on him, he was lying on his back with just the sheet over him. There was a huge mound in the middle. He winked at me and said, 'Sweetheart, I just wanted you to know the old man ain't dead yet.' I checked back a half an hour later and he was sleeping like a kitten."

JON FERGUSON

Jon Ferguson was born in October 1949 in Oakland, California, into a devout Christian family, much like his favorite philosopher, Friedrich Nietzsche. In fact, as a child, church services were held in the family living room. At age 17, his passion for sport was almost usurped by a keenness to save the world when he enrolled at Brigham Young University. Little by little, though, he realized that if Jesus couldn't do it, neither could he. His faith in divinity began to crumble. With an adieu to the US academic world where he'd been immersed in anthropology and philosophy – and with a desire to engage with the world at large – Ferguson hopped on a plane in 1973 and by chance ended up in Nyon, Switzerland where he was soon playing basketball in the top Swiss league, becoming a key player in what fans consider to have been the golden age.

Half a century later he is now just as well known for his writing (eighteen books published in French) as for his coaching (thirty years' worth). He won more games than any coach in Swiss basketball history, but he likes to remind people that he lost more than everyone else as well... He has written over twenty novels and a book on Nietzsche, Nietzsche au Petit Déjeuner ("Nietzsche for Breakfast") and a book on the history of Swiss basketball, Of Hoops and Men. For twenty-five years he also wrote a bi-weekly column in the Lausanne newspaper called "Ainsi Parla Schmaltz". His novel Farley's Jewel (Cinco Puntos Press, 1998) won a Barnes & Noble "Discover Great New Writers of America" prize.

Sign up for his publisher's newsletter at
www.jonfergusonbooks.com

Have you enjoyed *Adam's Cane*? Let us know by emailing
editor@hugejam.com

BOOKS BY JON FERGUSON

(Published by Huge Jam, 2022)

Adam's Cane
Foster's Depression
The Last Day Forever
Jesus & Mary
Mary & God
God & Naomi

Download 'The Last Day Forever' for free from the author's website
www.jonfergusonbooks.com

Out soon by the same author:

The Old Man and the Stone
Farmer's Daughter
Don't Bullshit Me Daddy
The Anthropologist

www.hugejam.com
www.jonfergusonbooks.com